12/22

HEART
FINDS

HEART FINDS

JAIME BERRY

LITTLE, BROWN AND COMPANY

New York   Boston

Little, Brown and Company
Hachette Book Group
1290 Avenue of the Americas, New York, NY 10104
Visit us at LBYR.com

First Edition: November 2022

Little, Brown and Company is a division of Hachette Book Group, Inc. The Little, Brown name and logo are trademarks of Hachette Book Group, Inc.

The publisher is not responsible for websites (or their content) that are not owned by the publisher.

Library of Congress Cataloging-in-Publication Data
Names: Berry, Jaime, author.
Title: Heart finds / Jaime Berry.
Description: First edition. | New York : Little, Brown and Company, 2022. | Audience: Ages 8–12. | Summary: Eleven-year-old Mabel is a quiet loner who only feels like herself when she is extreme treasure hunting with her grampa, but when her friendships start to crumble and her grampa suffers a stroke, Mabel must learn to let go of the past and embrace the future.
Identifiers: LCCN 2022035569 | ISBN 9780316390477 (hardcover) | ISBN 9780316390675 (ebook)
Subjects: CYAC: Collectors and collecting—Fiction. | Grandfathers—Fiction. | Change—Fiction. | Middle schools—Fiction. | Schools—Fiction.
Classification: LCC PZ7.1.B46346 He 2022 | DDC [Fic] —dc23
LC record available at https://lccn.loc.gov/2022035569

ISBNs: 978-0-316-39047-7 (hardcover), 978-0-316-39067-5 (ebook)

Printed in the United States of America

LSC-C

Printing 1, 2022

For my grandmother Stella, who was
my very first heart find

1

MY GRAMPA ALWAYS SAYS THE BEST TREASURES are the ones that hide in plain sight. That's what we search for—unnoticed, unwanted wonders. It takes a certain kind of skill to see something special in an item that's been tossed aside. We have to look with our eyes and our hearts. But when we do discover a hidden gem, it's like pure magic.

Today, the dumpsters outside the Old Creek Village apartment complex are a picker's heaven, relatively clean and stuffed to the brim. But Grampa and I, we don't see a dumpster at all—to us it's an oversize treasure chest. We're urban scavengers, modern-day pirates, only without the stealing. Mom calls it dumpster diving, but we think of ourselves as extreme treasure hunters. Plus, we don't actually dive into dumpsters. Grampa climbs in very carefully and only when he has to.

"Eureka!" Grampa shouts, shaking stray pieces of newspaper from a shoebox. "Full of cassette tapes and CDs. Can you imagine throwing away music?" This isn't really a question. It's more of a statement of disbelief.

People throw away all kinds of stuff. So really, I can imagine it, but I shake my head anyway. Grampa stands and passes the picking tool over to me. "Want a turn?"

"You know I do." I snatch the pole and use a milk crate as a stepstool. First, I poke a black Hefty, but it's a bit soupy, so I move on to a white bag pulled taut on the bottom in weird, angular edges. It's heavy and I lift it with a grunt over the edge of the dumpster, like pulling a giant catch from the ocean. Grampa says I have a "feel" for picking, knowing which bags to explore and which to avoid.

Dumpsters in Abner, Oklahoma, aren't like the

ones in the movies, full of puffy garbage bags waiting for people to fall into them from fire escapes. Nope. There've been some nasty surprises, a few with teeth, but we've also found a diamond ring, hardcover first editions of three books in the Nancy Drew series, and a table setting of genuine silver silverware worth almost five hundred dollars, even though the fork was bent.

I gently lower the bag and hear something solid as it touches the pavement. Untying the top isn't easy with dishwashing gloves on, but I can already feel it, that hum of excitement whenever a big find is nearby. Under an empty egg carton, I find a dusty wooden box. Once I lift it out and brush it off, I click open the hinged lid and a tangle of jewelry almost spills out.

"Whoa," I whisper.

Grampa comes over for a peek. He reaches in and takes something from the bottom while I try to unknot a mess of necklaces.

"What do you think?" Grampa holds up a small brooch, a fancy silver pin shaped like a spider. "I know jewelry's not your thing, but this one's kind of cool, right? There's another—a silver butterfly."

Grampa places the pin in my palm. I hold it close, turning it this way and that to see if it sparks anything in me. Just then the fading afternoon light flashes on the abdomen, and its leaf-green stone flickers. I nod and say, "I like it." I take the butterfly one for my best friend, Ashley, and slide it into my pocket.

He smiles at me and says, "Sometimes you don't find what you were looking for, but just what your heart needed."

Today, we've uncovered a crate full of lampshades, a table with only one broken leg, and two grocery bags full of what appear to be brand-new men's underwear. We believe that almost everything can be fixed. If it worked once, it can work again. But it's hard figuring out what to let go of and what to keep.

We won't be keeping the underwear.

I smile down at the little bug pin. The gemstone is smooth and solid, not plastic. Some fakes are easy to spot, some aren't. Maybe it belonged to a bug scientist studying the effects of venom. Or maybe a spy? Or some sort of secret double agent like Black Widow? Maybes are the best part of treasure hunting. Who knows what adventures that little spider's been on, and now, it'll be a part of mine. I stand a little straighter and then stare at Grampa.

He shakes his head. "Don't make me say it."

"Come on, Grampa." I work the pin through the fabric of my coveralls, shut the little clasp, and then look up at him again.

"All right, all right. You win catch of the day," Grampa admits. He peels off his gloves, ruffles my hair, and adds, "Don't let it go to your head."

Grampa resells most of what we find at Frank's Pawn and Salvage and donates the rest to his friend Archie, who owns the Tuesday Thrift. Some things we hang on to for our personal collections. And we're always on the lookout for heart finds, items that take hold and stir something in our hearts.

"You've got your first day of sixth grade tomorrow, and your mom will be by soon. Should we call it a day?" Grampa asks.

I look around at all our treasures. "Day's a weird name for all this stuff, but okay."

Grampa shakes his head. "I don't know whose jokes are worse, yours or mine." He nods toward the pin. "Decide to take her for a spin?"

"She'll keep some *eyes* out for me," I say. "My own personal *spy-der.*"

"Good one, Mae-mae." Grampa is the only person who calls me Mae-mae instead of Mabel, one more thing that's just between us. He puts a hand on my shoulder. "Looks good on you, but I hope it doesn't cause your life to *tailspin.*" I roll my eyes, as he thinks of another one. "Now, you've got your own *web*site!"

"Ha-ha," I say, but actually laugh a little too. "Your jokes are definitely worse."

During the summer, Grampa and I have a loose schedule. We don't always stick to it, but normally Monday is Frank's Pawn and Salvage followed by a taco dinner on Grampa's couch while viewing our favorite show, *Collector's Menagerie.* Tuesday is always a trip to the Tuesday Thrift, but we stop and visit with Archie whenever we have a donation. Wednesday means the Goodwill, sometimes a late afternoon hunt like today, then dinner with Mom at the Icon diner. Thursdays we look over our treasures from the week and plan for upcycling projects. Friday is our day of rest and relaxation. Weekends we reserve for repurposing our finds, taking what we've kept and giving them a new beginning.

We load our haul into the back of Grampa's pickup truck. Grampa closes the tailgate and texts Archie.

"He'll take the lampshades and the underwear." There's no telling what someone's heart needs most. Grampa starts the truck and says what he always does at the end of a good hunt. "Another day full of treasures." He doesn't just mean the finds, but our time together too.

Sometimes we don't keep anything at all. Those are what we call "dud days." We never know what a hunt holds, and that's what makes it so fun.

When we swing by the Tuesday Thrift, Archie's yellow truck is already there, and he stands out front waiting, dressed like he's ready for church. One of Archie's heart finds was a sketch of a banana, and he had no idea at the time that it would change his life. That's how heart finds normally work; you don't know what you have on your hands right away, but your heart has a clue—heart finds can connect you to a special person or a moment in time, or better yet, both.

Grampa stops and unloads. I lean out my window

and wave to Archie. "Hey, sweetheart," he says. "Find anything for your notebook today?"

"Not today," I say.

Grampa climbs back in with a handful of butterscotch candies from Archie.

Archie's find helped him fulfill a lifelong dream of opening his own secondhand store, where he takes donated items and keeps them until they call to someone else's heart. He writes heart-find stories from customers in a battered notebook by the register. So, I followed his example and started my own journal. I have one entry already.

Grampa and I stop by our storage space before we head to his house. His home is the shabbiest one in Lakehaven, the best neighborhood in our town. The neighbors don't quite appreciate Grampa's innovative decorating. His walkway is lined with the rims of broken plates, birdhouses built from scrap wood sit atop the rungs of a ladder, his fence is made from a few iron headboards that we painted yellow, two old colanders bursting with ferns hang over his porch, and his doormat is a coiled, recycled garden hose held together with zip ties. Everything is living out its second chance to the fullest.

Grampa and I exchange maybes about my pin all the way to the front door. Grampa nudges me. "Maybe it belonged to famous country singer and fellow Oklahoman Reba McEntire. That green gem would look fantastic with her red hair."

This is a pretty boring maybe, but Grampa has a thing for Reba, so I just nod. He frowns at my reaction and thinks of another. "Or maybe it belonged to famous outlaw Belle Starr. She lived in Eufaula and hid her outlaw friends in what's now Robbers Cave State Park. And when those fellas robbed stage-coaches, they took the passengers' jewelry."

As we walk in, I look down at my spider pin and say, "Now, that's a good maybe."

Mom's loading Grampa's dishwasher, wearing pink rubber gloves, an apron over her dress, and a deep frown. "Well, I'm glad you two came back empty-handed. There's hardly an inch to spare in this house."

Grampa and I exchange a quick look. Secret

keeping isn't my favorite thing, but Mom would put an end to a lot of our adventures if she knew all the details.

The storage space is one of the details Mom doesn't know. She pulls the gloves off, smacks them down on the counter, and scans me head to toe. I'm wearing the coveralls Grampa bought me. They are just like Grampa's, only his are faded and softer. Until now, Mom didn't know about the coveralls either.

She pinches the bridge of her nose. "Mabel, go change. You know we're going out for dinner." Grampa, Mom, and I eat together at the Icon diner once a week—our one family tradition.

While I'm latching my new pin to my T-shirt, I hear Mom's voice rise and I press my ear to the door. At first, I can't make anything out, but then I hear her say, "Different isn't always a good thing." Whatever Grampa says is impossible to hear. His voice is a low, steady rumble, like a box fan running at night.

I look down at my little pin and say, "Don't worry. They argue; they make up. That's how it works with Mom and Grampa."

I step out into a quiet hallway. "I'll clean up and

meet you two there," Grampa says, and gives me a wink—our secret signal that everything will be fine.

There's twice as much traffic because all the university students are moving back for the start of school. Mom grouches about Grampa the whole drive. "You know, when I was kid he was a workaholic, at the bank constantly. But now I guess he's just replaced one unhealthy obsession with another, filling the void… literally." Grampa worked at the Bank of Oklahoma, whose motto is "We go above. So you can go beyond." He retired and traded in his old BMW for an even older truck, but he still wears some of his bank T-shirts.

A car cuts Mom off and she yells, "Thank you very much!" This is part of what she calls her path to positivity, but mostly it seems like saying the opposite of what she means.

She finds a parking spot, turns off the car, looks over at my cargo shorts and Doc Martens, and takes a deep breath. "Let's have a nice night, okay?"

I wonder if when she has a bad night, she thinks it's my fault.

Benny and his husband, Otis, own the Icon. As soon as we walk in, Benny stands up from behind the front desk like he was waiting for us. He has a tall poof of black hair with silver on the sides, and he's also a fan of *Collector's Menagerie.*

"Jane and Mabel, my two beauty queens," he says, with his arms open to hug Mom.

Long ago, Mom was an actual beauty queen. She laughs like this is the best thing she's heard all day, but I roll my eyes. If Mom is anything to go on, beauty queens do not appreciate the pocket capacity of a good pair of cargo shorts.

"Benny, that was years ago," Mom says, and touches the pearl necklace she always wears. Her pageant days are long gone. Now, she works at Pattie's Parties as a wedding planner. But she's also a professional table-scaper, competitively designing and decorating these elaborate table settings. Her last year's county fair runner-up table was Dinner with Elvis. The plates looked like records and sat on a gold-flecked mirrored tabletop next to blue suede napkins. There's an Elvis table at the Icon, a Beyoncé booth, three tables featuring movie stars from black-and-white films I've never heard of, and more. Mom and Benny worked on the themes together.

Grampa comes in right after us and shakes hands with Benny. Then we go to our booth, the one dedicated to Princess Diana, and I slide in next to Grampa. Mom stares up at Princess Diana with her blond bob and pearl necklace and touches her own blond hair and pearls like she wishes she was looking in a mirror and not at a photograph.

Benny comes over for our order and says, "I read about a woman who bought a five-dollar painting at a thrift store because she thought it was so ugly that it'd make a perfect joke gift. Turned out to be a Jackson Pollock worth millions."

"Whoa," I say. "That's *Pol-lucky.*"

Benny laughs and says, "Mabel, you're the best kid I know."

Mom looks doubtful.

During dinner, Mom and Grampa do most of the talking. I study the spider pin, with its little white beads lining the legs and eyes made of shiny black stones. And there aren't just two eyes; there are eight, just like the real thing. A Sp-eye-eye-eye-eye-eye-eye-eye-eye-der. I smile, and when I look up Mom is frowning.

"Did you hear what I asked?" she says.

I shake my head. Her frown deepens.

"You'll be old enough for the Youth Division soon. So, I think we should do some tables together this year. You know, collaborate. I've got a few competitions coming up. What do you think?" She points her fork at me. "My tables are a little like a collection, you know." I raise my eyebrows and send Grampa a quick look. But Mom sees it and crosses her arms. "I don't appreciate being ganged up on."

"Now, Janie. Don't be dramatic." Grampa turns to me. "Might be fun."

I help Mom at competitions already and it's not even close to fun—colla*bor*ate, emphasis on the bore. Plus, when Mom creates a table, she spends months planning and polishing. Maybes and surprises are her worst nightmare.

"Interesting idea," I answer. This is something my fifth-grade teacher said whenever anyone said something way off.

Mom sighs and points to my shirt. "Is that pin something you found today?"

"Yeah," I say. "Like it?"

"It's different," she says, and gives me a tight smile.

Grampa looks up. "I think different is good."

Mom crosses her arms again just as Benny comes over with our food. "Enjoying your last days of summer, Mabel?"

"New year, new beginning. Right?" Mom asks. Mom has a thing for new beginnings from her one and only collection—self-help books. They're all about changing your life. *A New You: A Path to Internal Transformation*; *Beginning Again: The Fresh Start Within*; *The Magic of Beginnings*.

Grampa and I take bites of our burgers at exactly the same time.

I like my life just the way it is. And in my experience, new rarely means better.

2

THURSDAY MORNING, MOM'S HEAD IS COVERED with huge pink curlers in neat rows. She makes coffee in her robe, bunny slippers, and lucky pearl necklace. "I don't know why I keep buying you cute outfits if all you ever wear is a T-shirt, cargo shorts, and those boots."

I don't know why either.

"Where's Ashley?" Mom asks.

"We're meeting at the bus stop." I take a quick look at the spider pin I've attached to the small pocket of my backpack before I shove my new notebooks inside.

"How about I pick you up at Grampa's a little

early today? I have to develop a whole table concept for one of the campus sororities. We could get our tablescaping partnership started this afternoon." Mom wiggles her shoulders like she's dropping some really exciting news.

"Sure. Okay." I try to sound upbeat, but Mom's smile fades. I head to the bus already feeling like the day's gotten off to a stumbling start.

Over the summer, Ashley went to church camp, but instead of finding Jesus, she found Farrah Whitmore. Since she got home from camp all Ashley talks about is Farrah. Did I know Farrah has an older brother? Did I know Farrah's mom owns a beauty supply store? Don't I think Farrah Whitmore sounds like a movie star's name?

Ashley's full name is Ashley Enid Oostergooster. There are already three Ashleys in our grade, her Grandmother Enid is the meanest woman ever to ride a motorized wheelchair, and Oostergooster is... well, that one's obvious. My last name isn't much better—Cunningham—but it's got pun possibilities. So, the name fascination I sort of understand.

But then Ashley called to ask if we could meet

at the bus stop instead of walking together. It's an extra block for her to swing by my apartment. Maybe Ashley is too tired in the morning. Maybe she likes that time to think and wants to walk alone. But the one maybe I keep coming back to, is maybe she just doesn't want to walk with me anymore because she has a new best friend.

I sling my backpack around and decide to take the spider pin off and wear it. As I fasten it to my T-shirt, I whisper, "I could really use some help in the luck department today."

When I get to my stop at the corner of Cedar Street and Sycamore Lane, David Verdon, Kyle Colom, McKenna Higginbotham, and Ashley are waiting—all the usuals. And it's like nothing is different. Except for one thing. Farrah Whitmore is right where I usually am.

Ashley and Farrah wear matching hot-pink ankle socks and T-shirts that have ROCKSTARZ printed across the back. All sorts of things bother me about this situation, like maybe the reason Ashley isn't stopping by my house is that she's stopping by Farrah's instead. Rock stars is misspelled, and I'm pretty sure it's two words, not one. But the matching was definitely planned, and I wasn't included. So, I both deeply dislike their shirts and wish I had one on too.

It's very confusing and a whole lot of different for me to handle before eight AM.

"Guess what," Ashley says when I approach. "Farrah got a whole makeup set, with trays and trays of product."

The only product I know is the answer in a multiplication problem, and I'm not a fan.

"Want to come over after school today and try it out with me?" Farrah asks. It's possible she's asking both of us, but she looks mostly at Ashley.

"Can't. I have to go to my dad's." Ashley doesn't exactly look at me either, and the silence before my answer is long and awkward.

"Sorry, I can't either," I finally say. I don't give a reason because I don't have one.

When Ashley's parents got divorced at the start of the summer, she cried on the edge of my bed and asked me what it was like. I really didn't have a clue how to answer; my dad's never been around. He left before I was born. Every time I'd ask Mom about him she'd end up cleaning and buying a new outfit. She still says, "A cluttered house makes for a cluttered mind," which is maybe why Grampa's house makes her so upset.

Farrah nods to the spot on my shirt where the spider pin rests. "What's that?"

"A pin, actually a brooch. My grampa and I found it. Believe it or not, someone had thrown it away."

I turn so Ashley can see too. But she doesn't look. In fact, she avoids looking at me altogether. I must have said something wrong, but I don't know what.

"Did you at least wash it off?" Farrah asks.

"Of course," I say. But I didn't. Ashley doesn't say anything.

"It's his hobby. I just go along to help," I add. That's not exactly the truth, but it ends the conversation.

The bus rumbles up, and as soon as we climb on and I see the fourth row on the left empty, my seat all through elementary school, I feel better. Like always, I sigh and slide right in.

Ashley sits and we toss our bags on the floor space

between our feet and the seat in front of us, her purple bag next to my lime green one, like always.

Farrah's across from us, fourth row on the right, aisle side. Ashley scoots to the edge of our seat and turns to face her. This is not like always.

One stop goes by, and when the doors open, in walks a new boy. He has a tall stack of dark curls that fall over one side of his face, striped gym socks pulled up to his shins, pink Converse high tops, long cargo shorts, and glasses with bright red frames. As he walks down the center aisle, he doesn't look up from the thick book he carries.

"Cool shoes, man," David says. Judging from the laughter coming from his two friends, he means the opposite. Farrah breaks into giggles. But the new boy cuts his eyes at David and goes right back to reading.

I glance down at my own cargo shorts and Doc Martens, then stare at the floor. I unhook the pin, stick it back on the small pocket of my bag, and decide to leave Ashley's butterfly brooch where it is. Maybe mom was right. Different isn't good, especially in middle school.

The gem on my spider pin flashes in the light like it's winking at me. Today is sure feeling like a dud day, and I haven't even made it to school yet.

We rumble along Robinson Avenue, and I'm noticing all the things wrong on this bus. First off, it smells like a mixture of gasoline and the cheese section at Homeland. Then there's David, who picks his nose and shows his findings to Kyle before wiping them under the seat on aisle ten, right side. And there's Farrah. I lean forward to look at her. She wears lip gloss and little diamond earrings. No spider pins. No cargo shorts. No Doc Martens.

"Can you believe we used to call the bus the Deuce Caboose?" Ashley asks. Except she asks Farrah, not me. Deuce Caboose was my idea because it was bus number 2 all through elementary school.

Used to call, past tense, as in over and done. All of a sudden the view of Ashley's back causes a tickle in my throat like the beginning of a cry-knot. I swallow hard, but it doesn't go away.

We stop at the intersection in front of a small shopping center by the Shop-n-Save, and Farrah says, "Ugh. Look at that poor old guy digging in the garbage."

I see Grampa's truck before I see him. He has the tailgate down, using it as a step ladder. He's gripping the edge of the dumpster with one yellow rubber glove and using the other hand to pull out a big black Hefty bag.

"Gross. Bet he smells good," David says. A lot of kids laugh; even Ashley covers her mouth. David doesn't know that's my grampa. But she does.

That tickle in my throat turns into a sort of ache.

The light changes and our bus lurches forward. I want to say that Grampa *does* smell good, like lemon hand soap and coffee-roll donuts. But I don't say anything. My face is burning, and I grip the seat so hard I can feel the metal through the cushion.

Ashley looks down at my hands. She doesn't bump my shoulder with hers, tell David to shut up, or whisper "It'll be okay." Nothing.

Well, not really nothing. She shifts in her seat and doesn't meet my eyes.

Once we pull up to Alcott Middle School, my

tickly ache has turned to more of a boil. I walk straight off the bus, through the crowded hallways, with a printout of my schedule and my homeroom number, science with Mrs. Kirkpatrick in room 224. When I finally find it and sit, there are empty seats around me. Ashley makes her way to one across from me and says something about our lockers. I nod and smile, but really I'm still thinking about the bus.

Written on the whiteboard in looping cursive is the date and a fun fact.

This is the birth month of French naturalist Jean-Baptiste Lamarck, the first person to propose a full-blown theory of evolution.

Mrs. Kirkpatrick walks in wearing suspenders over a white button-down with her hair hanging in a straight, short bob. "Good morning, class. I thought the first day of middle school was a good day to talk about evolution and natural selection. Today, as an icebreaker, we'll play a few rounds of telephone. We'll get into our first official unit next week."

The boy in front of me raises his hand and asks, "What's natural selection? And what's telephone?"

I read *The Evolution of Calpurnia Tate*, so I could tell him natural selection has to do with how living things change over time to better adapt to their environments. But I don't. Mostly, I don't want to think about things evolving or me adapting or change of any kind.

"I'm going to whisper something to each person sitting in the front row." Mrs. Kirkpatrick walks over to the first chair closest to the door. "You'll turn around and whisper what you hear to the person behind you. And when we get to the back row, you'll say what you think you heard."

When I turn around and whisper, "Add outrageous grapes," which is what I'm pretty sure the boy ahead of me said, McKenna throws her head back and laughs out loud. Despite the heavy feeling from the bus ride, I smile. Once the round is over, we find out our original phrase was "advantageous traits," and the whole game was meant to illustrate how animals might evolve from one generation to the next.

There's a lot of laughing over what phrases we ended up with. I glance at Ashley; she stares straight ahead. Not long ago all it took was eye contact to give us the giggles. But not anymore.

3

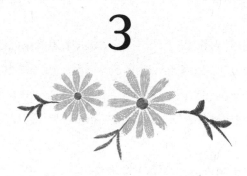

GRAMPA PICKS ME UP AFTER SCHOOL. I'M IN SUCH a rush to leave I almost plow over McKenna on the sidewalk, talking to the new boy with red glasses from our bus. She waves as I run past. Grampa waits in the line with all the other cars. I remember the laughter from the bus ride this morning and my face burns again. I hate how badly I want to leave before anyone recognizes his truck. But once I'm in the front seat, I look back and the new boy smiles and waves, and I suddenly don't feel so embarrassed.

"There's my girl," Grampa says as I buckle the seat belt. He looks me over. "Well, seems like you survived your first day without getting too banged up."

I nod, relieved that he can't tell how I feel. "It was okay. I liked my homeroom teacher."

Grampa studies me a bit longer. "What do you say we drive the loop? Relax and see if anything calls to us?"

"Cruising for catches?" I ask.

"Wandering for wonders," Grampa answers.

"Perusing for precious plunder."

"Well, I can't beat that." Grampa laughs and pulls out, and I already feel better.

Grampa and I have a long, lazy route we drive when we're not looking for anything in particular. We've snagged some great finds this way—a vintage beach cruiser bike (that's now mine), a working laptop (also mine), a handmade cedar chest (Grampa hung on to that one). But maybe my favorite was an old pedestal sink, just sitting out on the curb. It's now a bird bath in Grampa's backyard, an easy trash-to-treasure transformation.

We turn onto West Boyd and drive past the fire station. Since Grampa's AC has been broken for years, it's windows down in the summer. Grampa hangs one elbow out the window and steers with the other hand. The breeze blowing my bangs back is warm and relaxing, and I decide to try one of Mom's tricks. I take a deep breath in, then release it and all my stress out into the Oklahoma wind.

As we pass NAPA Auto Parts, Grampa slows the truck to a crawl. "Now what do we have here?"

A stack of four tires sits by their dumpster. One is frayed along the bottom and another is so worn the treads are almost completely gone. Grampa pulls in and kills the engine. "What do you think?"

"If we put something over the top, we could make foot cushions. Or stack two and use that glass tabletop we found last week for an outdoor coffee table?" I ask.

Grampa nods, but I know what's coming. "Or planters?" If it were up to him, all our finds would hold plants. "Still time to start a fall vegetable garden. If we swing by the Greenhouse off Highway 9, we could be genuine gardeners by sundown."

After an hour at the garden store, we're back in the truck and headed to Grampa's with a load of soil and the tiny beginnings of carrots, beets, broccoli, and red leaf lettuce. We turn into Lakehaven and as soon as I see Mom's car, I remember.

"Oh no," I groan.

As we pull into Grampa's driveway, Mom hops out and slams her car door. Before I can say sorry, she snaps, "I thought we had a plan. I've texted three times and been here waiting, in the heat I might add, for almost thirty minutes."

"Well, you could've gone in the house," I blurt.

"That's not the point, Mabel." Mom crosses her arms.

"With the first day of school, I just forgot."

Grampa starts unloading, staying out of the way. But Mom looks over at all our supplies. "Oh, I see. You and Grampa planned something else."

"Now, Jane. It slipped her mind. That's all," Grampa says.

Mom whips around. "Oh, believe me, Dad, I get it. I've had years of experience at being forgotten."

I don't know exactly what she's talking about, but by the way Grampa stares down at his boots, he does. She shakes her head. "Well, you two enjoy your project. I've got to go work on the Alpha Chi Omega table and floral design by myself, I guess."

Before Mom can get back in her car, I say, "Mom, I really am sorry."

Mom sighs and nods. "I'll be back to get you before dinner."

As her car pulls away, Grampa starts carrying the tires one by one to the backyard. He lays them out in a row a few feet in front of his back fence. I help, wiggling and rocking the last one into place.

Doesn't Mom realize the first day of middle school is a big deal—that maybe, just maybe, the world doesn't revolve around decorating tables? Wasn't she ever eleven?

Grampa goes to the truck and comes back with a bag of soil. He tears open the top and fills the first tire. He's never this quiet. Even though there was no yelling, whatever just happened between Mom and Grampa was a big deal too.

Grampa all bent over reminds me of the kids laughing at him this morning. And suddenly I'm not sorry. I'm mad. Mad at myself for ever feeling embarrassed and mad at Mom for upsetting Grampa and ruining our garden.

"So, that was a real blowout, huh?" *Blowout* can mean having a flat tire, but Grampa doesn't laugh. "I didn't want to do the table, but I didn't mean to forget. She's making such a big deal out of nothing."

"Want to start with broccoli?" Grampa asks. He's changing the subject. So, I sit and give him my best spill-it look. "Broccoli it is, then." He stands and walks off toward the truck.

We plant the broccoli all in one tire; not many will fit, but enough for the two of us. I realize I just left out Mom again and stop. "Why's this table stuff so important anyways? Why can't she have her thing and I have mine?"

After a second, Grampa stops too. "Go easy on your mom." He starts on the next tire and says, "You know your gramma used to say that Jane would grow even if she was planted sideways. She meant your mom was tough and she'd find a way to succeed no matter what was stacked against her. Maybe I'm one of the things she's had to overcome?" He laughs, but it's small and somehow unhappy.

Does he mean that Mom's embarrassed by his collecting? Grampa always gets this way when he talks about Gramma, and now Mom's made him even more depressed.

I use a trowel to make a space, squeeze a plant out of its container, gently pack the soil around the green leafy top, and then I reach over and put my hand on top of his. He looks up and smiles again. This time it's closer to his real one.

We spend the rest of the afternoon working on our new little garden, and by the time we're done, Grampa's back to his old self and the sun is hanging lower in the sky.

"It's a good start," I say, looking over our four new planters.

"I'm digging it," Grampa says, and shakes the trowel around.

"No contest. Your jokes are definitely the worst."

Grampa laughs and pats my back just as Mom pulls in to pick me up. Sometimes she comes inside and Grampa makes her a cup of tea. Today, she just honks the horn.

I take a few steps toward Mom's car, but then run

back and give Grampa a quick hug. He laughs and says, "See you tomorrow. I love you, Mae-mae."

"Love you too!" I yell over my shoulder and jog out to Mom's car. She gives me a tight smile as soon as I get in. We drive a few blocks without speaking. Then Mom clears her throat. "I'm sorry I overreacted. It was your first day of middle school, and I'm sure you had a lot on your mind. It really wasn't about you anyway."

"I'm sorry I forgot," I say. Mom nods.

The Cascades, the apartments where we live, is close by, but Mom is silent the rest of the way. She's still mad, so it feels like it's at least a little about me.

The slogan on our complex's sign says WHERE HOME MEETS AFFORDABLE LUXURY LIVING. The apartments aren't all that nice, for sure not luxurious, and just far enough from campus so the renters aren't college kids. And the truth is, it doesn't feel like home at all.

4

ALMOST THREE WHOLE WEEKS GO BY AND I'VE
sort of gotten used to Ashley's back facing me and to
the nervousness I feel every time my bus approaches
the intersection in front of the Shop-n-Save. But
after each final bell, I still run full speed to Grampa's truck. Every time I do it, I tell myself that it's
because I'm excited to see him and not that I'm hoping no one will see me. At least it's a Friday, because
I'm more than ready for some rest and relaxation.

Today, Grampa and I stop by Frank's Pawn and
Salvage to see if we can resell the camera we found
outside the Vintage Vantage, and then we swing

by Archie's. Archie once told us he opens the store whenever he feels like it, sometimes at night. So, you really never know what you might find at the Tuesday Thrift, even if that means you might find it closed.

Archie's truck sits parked out front, a sure sign he's working. We pull in and Grampa looks over at me. "Want to tell me what's bothering you lately?"

"It's just middle school. Switching classes, and so many more kids. There's hardly room to take a breath in the hallways. I don't know. I guess more has changed than I expected."

What I don't tell him is that I've felt funny about our collecting ever since that first bus ride, or that I asked Ashley to come over yesterday to do homework and watch TV together, but she said she couldn't because she was staying at her dad's, and he lives across town. It seemed to me that we could've easily come up with another plan, if she'd been interested.

Grampa nods and says, "Well, that's why we get along so well. Same old, same old works for us just fine. But I bet with some time, soon you won't even notice all the things bothering you now. What do you say we go in and see if Archie's come across anything special? Might cheer you up."

The Tuesday Thrift is right next to Joe's Diner, and there's always the faint scent of french fries in the air. I take in a deep breath, happy to find something familiar, and that's when I see a group of kids walking toward the new arcade across the street. David and Kyle from the bus are there, along with a few other kids I don't know. Farrah's with them and so is Ashley. It seems like she spots me too.

I freeze there in the parking lot while Grampa walks ahead. Then I hear David say, "Hey, isn't that the Junkman's truck?" He laughs and points. "And isn't that Mabel?" Ashley shrugs and looks away, as I turn and run for the door.

Normally I go straight to glassware and check whether anything new came in. Then I'll pick up each piece, close my eyes, and wait. Since a heart find might start off as just a flutter of a feeling, I try extra hard to notice. But nothing in Archie's calls to my heart; in fact, it's like my heart shrunk. Even Archie's hugs and butterscotches don't help.

Grampa ends up with a cracked bamboo fishing

rod and I leave empty-handed. He holds the rod up before putting it in the back of his truck. "What do you think?"

I look at it with my new raisin-size heart, and all I see is something old and broken. "Seems like it's in pretty bad shape."

Grampa inspects it again and says, "I like to think that sometimes things fall apart so we can take what's left and build something else, maybe even something better."

We rumble along and nothing feels right—even the warm breeze is like a hot breath in the face. Grampa drives past the Abner Municipal Office and there's a big banner advertising Fall Cleanup. Fall Cleanup happens every Sunday starting in September and runs through October. People can put almost anything on the curb Sunday evening and Sanitation will pick it up bright and early Monday. Last year, we found a violin, a full set of china, and an original Royal Classic typewriter missing only the *R* key.

Grampa bumps my shoulder, points, and starts singing the holiday song "It's the Most Wonderful Time of the Year."

When I don't respond, he asks, "You want to talk about it?"

I shake my head.

"What do you say I pick you up early before school Monday morning and we hit the road and see what treasures Fall Cleanup has to offer?" he asks. "I'll clear it with your mom."

I nod.

"Want to come by and see our garden? Everything looks good except the beets. Hey, maybe I should become a musician." Grampa looks over at me.

I shake my head again. "Don't say it."

"Because of my sick beets." I groan and Grampa laughs.

I laugh a little too. But then I hear David and think about Ashley's reaction and feel small and awful all over again.

"Actually, Grampa, I think I might have a cold or something. I just want to go rest."

"Sure thing, Mae-mae." Grampa drops me home, and I spend the rest of the weekend sulking and dreading Monday. Sunday evening, I text Grampa and tell him I still feel bad and that I can't go treasure hunting in the morning. It's the first time I've ever skipped out on a hunt and lied to Grampa.

·᠊ᠥᠵᠥ᠊·

The next morning, even though I'm barely awake, I'm replaying what happened outside the Tuesday Thrift. I flop over and lay flat on my back, hoping that the guilt from lying to Grampa might quit wrestling around in me if I'm still and quiet. I'll see him after school and we'll drive the loop again and it'll all be fine.

My collection of vintage glass baskets sits on my windowsill. My favorite, a marbled red one, is a Tiara Indiana Glass Sunset Amberina Constellation Basket. It's a long name for such a small thing. The cuts in the glass create four-pointed stars, and the base is a deep burgundy that shifts to red and then orange before fading to a golden amber on the handle. On the bottom are the tiny initials TJ, put there by a real person, not a machine.

The colors from my baskets flicker in the day's first light. When the sun hits them right, slow streaks of yellow, orange, pink, and red spread across my legs. The constellation cuts make little prisms of light here and there all over my comforter. I imagine it's like sleeping in a sunset-colored rainbow.

I got my Amberina basket early on in my collecting. Since then Grampa's taught me it's more fun to fill in the details with what he calls our right to historical whimsy. Mom calls it making stuff up.

But I think the maybes are one of the best things about our hunts. Who knows where my little basket was before it became mine. Maybe it held the jewelry of someone exceptional like Wilma Mankiller, the first female chief of the Cherokee Nation. I told Mom this, and she said it also looked about the right size to hold a set of false teeth.

I'm staring at my Amberina legs and thinking about Grampa, when Mom walks into my room without knocking. She's still in her robe, and her face is flushed like she's been crying.

A cloud passes over the sun and for a second my Amberina legs are plain old comforter-covered legs.

"Mabel, it's Grampa. He's had a stroke." She picks at the knotted belt of her robe.

I hear the words but can't figure out what she means because it doesn't make any sense. Grampa's fine. He has to be fine. I grab my comforter and pull it up toward my chin. Mom sits on the end of my bed and puts her hand on my leg.

Maybe he's okay? Only one good maybe, and all the bad maybes roll in like a summer storm.

"Oh, Mabel," she says. "He'll recover, but I can't quit thinking about him lying there alone for goodness knows how long." Mom starts to sob hard enough to shake my bed. She doesn't run for tissues or cover her face or fuss with her running mascara. I sit there, holding on to my comforter and that one good maybe and then what Mom is saying sinks in.

Grampa went on the Fall Cleanup hunt by himself. He went out in the darkest part of the morning to search for something amazing without me, without me because I lied and stayed here in bed instead of going with him.

Mom's leaving out the most important detail of all.

Grampa wasn't supposed to be alone. He was supposed to be with me.

5

I DON'T GO TO SCHOOL THAT MORNING AND INSTEAD stay with Mrs. Hammons from next door while Mom goes to the hospital. She's gone for three hours and twenty-four minutes, and the whole time I feel like I've got a shaken-up Coke in my chest ready to explode. When Mom gets back, I make us peanut butter and jelly sandwiches for lunch.

"Are you sure you want to go?" she asks between bites.

"Of course I'm sure." Mom always says talking with confidence can actually make a person *feel* confident. It was worth a try.

We stop by Grampa's house on the way to the hospital. On the drive there, Mom warns me that Grampa's not exactly like his old self, that he has some trouble talking, that his body isn't moving quite right, that he'll need help with his recovery. None of the things she tells me to be prepared for are good things.

She cuts the engine and says, "Let's see if we can find a few things Grampa can use in all his mess of stuff."

From the street, no one would guess how many treasures are tucked away inside Grampa's house. His hallways are lined with shelves made from dresser drawers and filled with his collections. Usually, I think of Grampa's house as sort of like my one big heart find; no place on earth speaks to my heart so clearly.

Every object has a place and a reason for being there. Even his "miscellaneous" shelf has a certain kind of order. A stack of old horseshoes, a row of mason jars filled with his glass marble collection, a small brass fawn, three antique thimbles. It's my favorite because what each item has in common is that it doesn't fit in anywhere else and still Grampa loves it.

Grampa's room used to be Mom's when she was a kid. The door to the room he shared with my gramma stays closed. I've only peeked in once. All my gramma's stuff is still there, her dresser covered in perfume bottles, a dress hanging in front of the closet door that she intended to wear, and her shoes at the foot of the bed.

Mom pulls an old pair of slippers from Grampa's closet. His shoe rack is made from sawed-off plastic pipes we found by the dumpster at the Home Depot and looks sort of like honeycomb.

"Good idea," I say. "He loves those."

"Well, he needs something with no laces." Mom inspects them. "We'll get him some new ones tomorrow."

"But he loves *those*." I take the slippers from her and shove them in the bag. She shrugs and moves on to Grampa's dresser.

"You know some things outlive their purpose—those slippers are a good example." Mom pauses and points over to the nightstand, where a fishbowl sits half filled with Grampa's spare change. "That was my fishbowl when I was a little girl. I thought my goldfish lived ten years but turned out your grampa replaced that fish nine times without my knowing." Mom shakes her head and looks toward Gramma's room. "Sometimes you have to have hard conversations and let go to get over something. And sometimes it's nice to get over something together."

Mom complaining about Grampa is nothing new, but it seems like she could give him a pass today.

"Why no laces?" I'm afraid I already know, but I'd like a change of topic.

"The right side of his body is weak, and he'd need both hands, so..." Mom trails off.

While she was at the hospital, I did some research. Nothing about a stroke is even a little bit whimsical. Oxygen is carried through the bloodstream to the brain. Strokes stop blood flow and that can cause about two million neurons to die. It's like Grampa's brain was being smothered.

"Did he have a sudden headache?" I ask.

Grampa shouldn't have been alone. If he hadn't been by himself, then I'd know the details. Maybe if I knew the details then I wouldn't have this growing heavy feeling inside. Maybe I could have helped. And the most awful maybe of all, if I'd been there like I was supposed to be, maybe it wouldn't have happened in the first place.

"I don't know, Mabel. I wasn't there." Does she mean that *I* should have been? I whip around to look at her, but she's still going through Grampa's drawers. "The preacher at the Presbyterian church found him unconscious just off Avondale Drive.

"This is the worst possible time for this to happen. I've got the Home and Garden Show coming up, regionals the next month, and if I qualify, the Expo after that. This is like my Mardi Gras nightmare table all over again." Mom pinches the bridge of her nose. "Not to mention, the extra expenses." She stops folding sweatpants and looks over at me. "See if Grampa has any clean socks."

I pull the wooden drawer out and toss pairs of socks into the bag. How can she think of competitions right now?

"Grampa will have to stay at the hospital for a while, then he'll be discharged and transferred to an assisted-living facility. I've been looking into one called Whispering Pines. Professionals will figure out what therapy he'll need and let us know when they think he's able to live on his own."

My grip tightens around a roll of socks. "Well, there are these things called cluster headaches that can mimic the symptoms of a stroke. Maybe it was that?"

"The doctor is sure it was a stroke. And, Mabel, you have permission to look up your glassware facts online, not random health issues." Mom saying my name means she's irritated. She folds a fourth pair of sweatpants, working her way toward a mountain of athleisure wear. I know about athleisure wear thanks to Ashley, who is all about it, but she leans more toward the leisure part and less toward the athletic part.

"Well, maybe..." I start.

"Mabel, enough maybes," Mom says. "Why don't you find something you think Grampa would like to have in his room?"

Normally she isn't full of good ideas, but this is one. I know exactly what to take.

Dr. Jonathan Handsome is a two-foot-tall rooster carved from pine, possibly from a fence post, dating back, we think, to the nineteenth century. My gramma bought Dr. Jon the same day I was born. She cut short a Florida vacation with her sister because I came early. The doctor who delivered me was named John Hanson.

Gramma drove all the way from Dunedin, Florida, with the rooster rolling around in her trunk, so hers could be one of the first faces I saw. The rooster's named after my delivery doctor and I'm named after her. Dr. Jon ties us all together, me and Grampa, and Gramma, and he's one of Grampa's heart finds. Grampa has a few others, but Dr. Jon is his favorite—top of the pecking order.

"Mabel, what's going on in there?" Mom asks.

Mom comes into the living room where Grampa keeps all his large sculptures grouped under the window right next to the side table of stacked vintage suitcases.

"Oh no. Mabel, we can't bring that big old chicken," Mom says.

"He's a rooster." I have to sit Dr. Jon down so I

can cross my arms and give her a look. Mom sighs. Victory!

On the way to Abner Regional Hospital, Mom goes over what I should expect again.

"He's a little bruised, he's got some right-side paralysis, and speech is also a bit of a struggle for him right now. But all the doctors say these are things that with time and therapy will get much better." And I listen—really, I do. But when I walk into Grampa's room, what I see is so much worse than what I expected.

Mom sits Dr. Jon on the nightstand. I toss the duffle bag packed full of Grampa's sweats into a pink chair.

"Hi, Dad," Mom says. "Look who's here."

Mom is talking about Dr. Jon. But Grampa looks at me. He has a big scrape on the top of his cheek and another on his forehead; both are surrounded by bruising. One eye is swollen shut.

"There's my girl," he says. Only it sounds more like "Airs my Earl." He tries to smile, but just one side of his mouth lifts.

I focus on the chair—it's covered in a rose-colored

plasticky leather, and nothing like the soft, worn recliner in Grampa's living room. Not a lot of maybes around that chair.

When I finally look up at Grampa, he tries to wink, our sign. But he can't quite do it.

One tear escapes, and I quickly wipe it away. Mom said he'd get better with time. How much time? He looks so far away from his old self, so far away from better.

"Hey, Grampa," I say. He reaches out his left hand and I take it. He gives my hand a squeeze.

Mom talks the whole time we're there, and I keep my eyes on the TV.

"I think he's pretty worn out," Mom whispers.

When I look at Grampa his eyes are closed. "Bye, Grampa," I say. His eyelids raise slowly, like even their weight is hard for him to lift. He barely moves his left hand in the tiniest of waves, and I duck out of the doorway so he won't see me cry.

Mom wraps her arm around me. "We have to give it some time." I lean my head into her shoulder, and we walk like that, in a little huddle, all the way out to the car.

That night we order takeout and move vases, silk flowers, multiple place settings of dishes, and piles of fabric—all the supplies for Mom's upcoming table—so we can sit together.

"Grampa has a hard recovery ahead of him. But with our support, he can do it." Mom gives me a hard stare. "I think Oprah said nothing helps as much as helping someone else. And Grampa will need our help."

I half listen while Mom talks. When she says that Grampa will need full-time care for a while I start whole listening.

"One of the things we might need to consider is listing Grampa's house. He may not be able to return to living alone." Mom takes a bite and stares off into the living room, like getting rid of Grampa's house is no big deal.

"Sell Grampa's house?" I ask. "What about his collections?"

Mom sighs. "We're talking worst-case scenario, but things will have to change. I'm not sure how long it will be before he can drive again. Plus, we could use the extra money for the care he'll need."

"But Grampa loves his collections," I say. "I read that after a stroke sometimes people get depressed. Won't getting rid of all the stuff he loves make him more depressed?"

Mom shoots me a look and turns away for a minute, then she says, "I know you love your grampa. I do too. I've got some tough decisions to make, but the hardest choices can sometimes pave the way forward." This is definitely something from one of Mom's self-help books. "Understand?"

I nod, but I don't understand. "Isn't figuring out how to take care of Grampa so he could go home and keep his collections the hard decision and sending him to a place where other people will take care of him the easy one?"

Mom sighs. "Okay, Mabel. Grampa's going to Whispering Pines, an assisted-living and recovery center for seniors. His insurance will pay for most of it and his savings will pay for the rest, while it lasts. Hopefully, he won't need to be there long. But once he's discharged, we run into another problem. Where Grampa lives, Lakehaven, has the highest property tax in all Cleveland County. His groceries probably run around two to three hundred, plus utilities are another couple hundred. His Social Security check will cover most of that, but Medicare will only pay for a portion of his outpatient care—occupational, physical, and speech therapy. Grampa doesn't have that much extra money coming in every month, and neither do we. I don't have a good handle on the numbers yet, but I think I can cover things as they are for a few months. That's it."

I don't understand a lot of what she says. But it sounds like a lot of money and not a lot of time.

"Want to know any more of the details?" Mom asks. I shake my head.

"If it's about making money, I can do some hunts to help out," I say.

Mom starts shaking her head before I finish talking. "Absolutely not. I don't like it to begin with, but I certainly won't have you digging through trash alone." She sighs again. "Some things you just have to let grown-ups handle."

Before I go to bed that night, Ashley sends me a text: Sorry about your grampa. Mom must have told her mom. I sort of hate how much better it makes me feel to hear from her.

I take my Amberina basket from the window-sill and as I turn it this way and that, I think about Grampa and his drooping face. I think about how hospital rooms don't have fireplaces or space for miscellaneous shelves. I think about how much collecting means to Grampa. And I decide he's had enough taken away.

Even though I don't really want to, I think about Ashley too. If everything can be fixed, why can't this? Getting Grampa back home and sorting out my friendship with Ashley won't be easy. But if Grampa's taught me anything, it's how to take things that look a mess and make them right again.

6

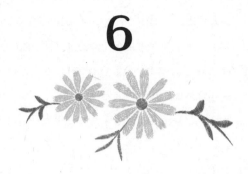

TUESDAY MORNING, MY FIRST THOUGHT IS THAT Grampa and I can go to the Tuesday Thrift after school, and then my second hits like a punch in the stomach— Grampa's still in the hospital. Mom lets me stay home another day, and we go back by Grampa's to get his pillow and a blanket from his bed. "I'm going to swing by the CVS and print out some pictures of you two for his room and grab him some earplugs. Are you sure you're up for helping Archie?" she asks once we're back in the car.

I nod. "He's counting on me. I think I'd feel worse if I didn't do it, and I'm sure Grampa would want me to." She pulls up to the Tuesday Thrift and parks. Grampa and I always work with Archie on his window displays. I do want to help Archie, but the whole truth is the idea of seeing Grampa in the hospital again makes my stomach feel twisty.

Mom smiles and honks a goodbye as I walk across the parking lot. When I open the doors, Archie's not in his usual spot at the register, and I have a minute to look around by myself.

At the start of each aisle is something strange and amazing—items that have what Archie calls the "wow factor." This week there's a barrel painted to look like a Campbell's Soup can, a vintage grocer's scale, a chair with rabbit ears, and a three-foot-tall vase shaped like a dress with a bouquet of fake flowers sitting where the head should be. Like Archie says, you never know what will call to a person's heart.

The front window is behind a little gate, and there's a short set of stairs, sort of like a stage. It's still set up with the same scene we created last time. Each of the mannequins is wearing a swimsuit and sunglasses. Over to the side are two beach towels and a basket stuffed with some plastic fruit.

Archie named the mannequins Regina and Carl.

Regina has on a wig that someone dropped off and Grampa couldn't resist wearing it the whole time we worked—he looked 100 percent ridiculous. When he climbed the ladder to hang a beachball so that it looked like it was in midair, he said, "I can't see a thing with these bangs in my eyes." Archie laughed so hard he had to sit down.

"Regina is forever going to remind me of your grampa now." Archie walks out from the back room. I give him a hug, and he says, "You didn't need to come today, but I'm sure happy to see you." He holds me out at arm's length. "Bobby's as tough as a steel-toed boot. I know he's going to be okay. How are you and your mom doing?"

"We're good. Mom's going to pick me up in a little while, and we'll head to the hospital. But I thought I'd stop by here and help you with this window. Not really swimsuit season anymore," I say.

"What do you say we set up a football-themed window. Dress them in team colors and even put out a TV I just unloaded in the storeroom?" Archie asks.

I nod and we get to work. Without Grampa it's harder than usual, but Archie and I manage to take everything down. While I try to put a pair of crimson-and-cream-checked pants on Carl, which is more difficult than it sounds, Archie looks over and says, "You never know what's going to be special for someone. Take those pants, for instance."

I laugh and he finds a pair of pom-poms for Regina. Archie brings a small console and a TV that is so old it's not anywhere near flat. It takes all my strength to help him position the loveseat. But by the time we're done, we've created a little living-room scene.

Archie pulls a real cloth handkerchief from his shirt pocket, wipes his brow, and hands me a butterscotch. We unwrap our candies, pop them in our mouths, and look at our window for a minute. Butterscotches from Archie give me the same feeling my Amberina basket does.

"Something's not right. Just a minute." I run off down one of the aisles and come back with a book and a pair of reading glasses. Archie works on posing Carl so that it looks like he's reading.

We step back again. Archie nods and says, "Football's not for everyone. What do you say we take a photo and send it to your grampa?"

"He's going to be okay." I didn't mean to say it out loud, but as soon as the last word leaves my mouth my eyes fill with tears.

Archie puts his arm around me. "I know he is, sweetheart." He shakes his head and nods toward Regina. "You know, someone wanted to buy that hairpiece and I said no. Couldn't bring myself to let go of it yet. Not sure if I'd call that wig a heart find, but it's funny how things work, isn't it? I wonder if maybe some heart finds are temporary, like they remind you of a moment for as long as you need it."

Archie gives me a hard stare. "Your grampa has been through worse. He'll get through this too. And this time he'll have us to help him."

I nod as Mom pulls in. "I have an idea." I walk over to Regina and lift the wig off her head. "Mind if I borrow this? I'll bring it back on our way home."

"Not at all." Archie looks over at bald Regina and says, "Oh Lord, now she looks even more like your grampa."

The wig earns a frown from Mom and a couple of long stares at the hospital, but it's worth it when I walk into Grampa's room. At first he doesn't notice because I stand behind Mom, but when he does, he laughs loud and hard.

He doesn't try to talk the whole time we're there, so Mom takes all that quiet and fills it with chatter about her upcoming table. When we leave, he pats my back with his left hand and says, "Love you, Mae-mae."

"Love you too, Grampa." But it's so hard for him to say those three words that I end up crying on the way home.

Mom looks over at me. "Why are you crying? You got him to laugh for the first time since he's been admitted. You did good today."

I try to smile. But maybe helping others only helps if you don't feel like you caused the problem in the first place.

7

GRAMPA STAYS A WHOLE WEEK AT ABNER REGIONAL Hospital. Monday while I'm at school, Mom works on getting him discharged and admitted into Whispering Pines. I spend the day in a sort of daze. By last period, all I'm thinking about is Grampa living somewhere other than his own house. Even if it is temporary, it still feels wrong to me.

Mom picks me up, gives me a quick hug, and asks, "Ready to go see your grampa's new digs?"

New digs? Mom thinks being positive is a problem-solving strategy.

"Sure," I say.

She nods. "Change your mindset, change your mood."

On the way to Whispering Pines, we pass a small strip mall. I notice a handwritten going-out-of-business sign—EVERYTHING MUST GO. THIS SUNDAY. If Grampa were home, we'd hit their dumpster hard. Most stores throw out all the stuff they can't get rid of after a final sale. This would be strictly a trash-to-cash score. Grampa's usually not into hunts for the money, but it's sort of thrilling.

This coming Saturday Mom has a competition, but on Sundays when Grampa and I don't have a project planned, we go on hunts. I'm not about to give it up. Besides, Mom didn't say I couldn't go at all; she said I couldn't go alone.

I pat the pocket of my T-shirt, where the spider pin is latched inside, my last big find. I've been wearing the pin like that all week, out of sight but close to my heart. Sometimes I even wish on it, though that's not really helped much. The last time Mom and I visited Grampa at the hospital he was pretty much the same, and Ashley still sits facing Farrah. But maybe a big find would be just the kind of luck I need.

·~᪲᪲᪲᪲~·

The first thing about Whispering Pines that bothers me is there are no pine trees, not even any cedars. There's only a short row of bushes trimmed into little spheres, like leafy meatballs. And the whispering isn't meant to be taken literally, but still, puny shrubs do not whisper in the wind. I know a name isn't always factual, but this name seems more like a trick.

Mom parks and says, "Tell me one good thing." This is something she read in one of her books, *The Gratitude Attitude.* She puts her hand on mine. "I'll go first. Grampa's prognosis is good. He'll get better."

"It's not far from our house, which means I can bike or walk here to visit," I say.

Mom smiles and squeezes my hand before we get out and walk into the lobby. It's sort of like a hotel, except there's another set of doors that we have to be buzzed through by a lady in mint green scrubs sitting at the front desk.

"Why do they keep those doors locked?" I ask.

"So the residents with dementia can't wander out and get lost," Mom says.

"Can Grampa leave whenever he wants and come back?" I ask. I learned about dementia when I researched strokes; it's like confusion, sometimes it comes and goes, and sometimes it's permanent. It was one of the things we were lucky Grampa doesn't have.

"Not yet," Mom says. "But he'll get day passes soon. The doctors at the hospital don't think he'll need to stay here more than a few months." Mom signs in at the front desk and shows her driver's license.

On the walk to the elevator, Whispering Pines starts to feel a lot less like a hotel and a lot more like a fancy jail. The elevator opens and there's a man asleep in a wheelchair. A woman with blond hair pulled in a high, tight bun dressed in the same shade of mint green stands behind him. She smiles at me. "Nice day, huh?"

She pushes the man into the lobby, parks his chair in a square of sunlight shining through the sliding doors, and as the elevator closes, I hear her say, "Look, Mr. Feddrel, the sun is out."

Mom punches the button for Grampa's floor and says, "See? The staff here is great. They're really kind to the residents. Even when they're asleep. I've been here a few times now, and with each visit I like it more. I think it's going to be really great for Grampa." She winks at me. I try to smile, but my lips are stuck.

Grampa's room is on the second floor. There's a nurses' station right by the elevator. One of the residents stands near the counter with her walker to the side. She's wearing gray sweatpants, like the ones mom brought for Grampa, but has on fancy sneakers, not slippers—Adidas with metallic stripes.

The nurse at the counter says, "Good morning again, Jane. Your dad is all settled in. His room is the third one on the left." She points down a hall.

Mom smiles and nods. The hallways are wide and empty, but there are a lot of smells, some lemon fresh and some vanilla, but all artificial, like they came straight from an aerosol can. There are fake floral arrangements on tables, and everything is pale pink and seafoam green. It's not just that there's no clutter; there's no personality. Nothing in Whispering Pines is like Grampa's house.

We stop outside room 217. "Grampa doesn't even like pastels that much," I mumble.

"Mabel, an open mind opens doors." Mom grabs my hand and pulls me forward.

Grampa's room at Whispering Pines is a little bigger than his hospital room. It has two beds and a small set of drawers divided down the middle, with a narrow closet on each end. There is a TV mounted between two big windows, and there's Mr. Curtis.

Mr. Curtis is a tall man with gray hair only around the bottom of his head, circling a shiny brown scalp. He gets up and moves smoothly toward the door. "Nice to see you again, Jane. And who's this young lady?"

I don't answer. Mr. Curtis seems happy and totally fine, like he could go home tomorrow. For some reason, looking at him makes the tightness in my throat ache a little harder.

"This is my daughter, Mabel," Mom says. "This is Mr. Curtis, Grampa's roommate."

"Call me Walt. Well, I'll leave you alone. Robert should be back any minute. He went for his first session with Ms. Amanda."

Robert is my Grampa's first name. His friends, like Archie, call him Bobby.

Grampa's bed is empty, but the blanket is pulled up tight with the sheet folded down at the top. I wonder who made it for him and how he feels about someone else touching his sheets, not even his regular sheets.

"Doing okay?" Mom asks me. "Amanda is Grampa's speech therapist. She's nice. You'll like her."

The door to Grampa's room opens. He's being pushed in a wheelchair by a lady with thick braids and lots of earrings, even one in her nose. She has a megawatt smile that instantly makes me feel a little better.

Grampa's bruises have faded to a pale greenish shade. When he sees me, he smiles, and I focus on his eyes. His eyes are maple syrup brown and crinkled at the edges, same as always.

Mom hugs him. He only lifts his left arm and pats her back. Mom looks over at me like I should hug

Grampa too, but I'm afraid if I do I'll start to cry. "Hi, Grampa."

"Hi," he says. His *hi* is long and drawn out.

The Amanda woman gives me a different smile, a softer one that says she knows how hard this is.

"Hi, Mabel, I'm Amanda. Your mom thought you might like to meet with me to talk about your Grampa Robert's therapy. He's doing great. It's good for him to use his voice as much as possible, but saying a lot is hard work for him right now. It'll take patience from everyone, and I can teach you all some strategies to help. Not now, but whenever you're ready."

Grampa nods at me a bunch. He definitely seems better than he did at the hospital, where he was always in bed and not in the mood to do anything but watch TV. Mom looks like she might start crying, so I force out, "Sure. That'd be great."

"For the most part, he'll be able to talk with you like he normally would, but when he has a lot to say, this might help." She holds up something that looks a little like a banged-up tablet reader. "It's old but it works, and I don't think he'll need it for long. He's already made quite a bit of progress." She moves so she can see Grampa. "In the meantime, do you all have any questions for me?"

When will he be able to hug with both his arms? When will his smile spread to his whole mouth and not just be in his eyes? When will he come home?

But I don't ask any of my questions. Instead, I just shake my head and try really hard to smile again.

Mom says, "Sorry." I'm not sure what she's apologizing for.

Amanda laughs. "I have a son the same age. Believe me, I'm used to one-syllable answers. He just started school here. Maybe you've seen him? I learned from your mom that we don't live too far away from each other."

I shrug, and Amanda and Mom share another look and then laugh.

They start talking, and Grampa is staring at me. When Amanda turns to leave and waves, Grampa is still studying my face. It's like he's hoping that I'll understand what he wants to say but can't. I concentrate on his eyes, but I can't hear his thoughts.

"I'm sorry, Grampa." I mean I'm sorry about not being able to read his mind, but then other things I'm sorry for sneak in. Grampa's eyes are not smiling anymore. And then I'm sorry for making him sad. I can't cry in front of Grampa; he's got enough to worry about.

"I'll be right back," I say, push past Mom to get to the hallway, and close Grampa's door. For a few minutes I stand just outside, taking deep breaths and trying to keep tears away again. Mom talks but I can't make out what she says. Then the electronic voice from Grampa's device rings out loud and clear, "Don't use that money for this. We've got at least a month to decide."

The way Grampa's device doesn't sound a bit like him only makes me want to cry more. I don't feel right listening in, so I walk back toward the nurses' station. What money are they talking about? Are they talking about Grampa's house? Or money to pay for here? Mom said she could afford the extra expenses for a few months, but Grampa just said a month. A month, and then what?

Sometimes the actual facts help keep all the bad maybes away. While I was at school, I read online there are ten things that cause almost all strokes. Real causes, not imagined ones.

1. High blood pressure.
2. Stress.
3. Depression.
4. Heart disorders.
5. Bad cholesterol.

I stop halfway through the list and think. Grampa drinks a ton of coffee, which can cause high blood pressure. Maybe he was extra stressed because I wasn't with him. Grampa is definitely still sad about Gramma. Maybe a broken heart is the same as a heart disorder? And maybe we've eaten *too* many tacos.

All I've convinced myself of is that Grampa's stroke is even more my fault than I thought before. I plop into one of the plastic chairs by the nurses' station, rest my head in my hands, and lift my pocket open so that I can make some eye-to-eight-eye contact with my spider pin. "If you're lucky at all, I'm really not seeing it," I whisper. I startle when someone sits beside me.

The new boy with the red glasses from the bus holds his hands up. "Sorry," he says. "My mom made me come over. She's one of your grandfather's therapists."

He's walked down the center aisle of our bus with his head buried in a book for weeks. But up close I notice his pink high tops have lime green laces, and his shirt has an electron and the words "Because You Matter." He also has a very nice smile, just like his mom.

I look down the hallway and Ms. Amanda quickly pretends to be filling out paperwork on a clipboard.

"She thought you might want to talk to someone." He smiles. "I'm Jasper, also known as the New Guy."

"Your shirt's a pun," I blurt.

He nods and smiles wider. "I know."

"What are you reading?" I don't feel like talking about Grampa with a stranger.

He holds it up. "This is *Endling: The Last* by Katherine Applegate. It's about Byx. She thinks she may be the last of her species, so she teams up with an unlikely but adorable sidekick and they go on a quest to find more of her kind."

"Sounds good," I say.

"It is." He holds it out to me so I can see the cover.

There's an awkward quiet before he says, "So,

the bus drops me here instead of at home in the afternoons. I met your grandfather earlier. He's nice."

"Well, I hope he doesn't stay here long. I don't mean to be rude, but I just want him back home."

"Right." Jasper nods. "He lives with you?"

"No, but we spend almost every day together." A man walks the halls pushing a rolling bin, collecting trash from the rooms. He and Jasper exchange a wave. Since Grampa's been in the hospital, my afternoons have been full of horrible bus rides, homework, and TV until Mom gets off work. No Grampa, no routes, no treasure hunting. Then I remember the sign I saw on the way over.

"Well, I'll let you get back to…whatever you were doing." I feel my cheeks flush, knowing he must have seen me whispering into my pocket. "Truth is, I think my mom made me come over because she's worried I won't make friends with anyone but the residents." He turns to walk away. If he saw me talking to my shirt and he's not freaked out, maybe he doesn't scare easily. I pat my pocket again. Maybe this little pin is finally working its magic. Maybe Jasper's just who I need.

"Wait. What are you doing next Sunday, late afternoon?" I ask.

His eyes widen. He probably wasn't expecting an invitation to go anywhere.

"Here's the deal. Grampa and I normally go on scavenging hunts, but it's a two-person job. I need a partner."

Jasper's eyes widen. "Sort of like a quest?" He holds up his book. "And you need an unexpected and adorable sidekick?"

I laugh. "Sort of. I need you to stand watch while I—"

"I'm in," Jasper says. "This is the first interesting thing that's happened since I moved here."

Jasper and I exchange phone numbers just as Mom steps out of Grampa's room and waves at me to come.

"I'll text you the location."

"I'll be there," he says.

I walk back down the hall, only this time I don't feel weighed down by all the ways this place isn't like Grampa's. This time I practically skip, lifted by the idea that he'll be back home in no time. If money is the problem, then I can help. Trash to cash is different than searching for heart finds, but sometimes practical beats whimsy.

I stick my head in Grampa's room. He's lying down, his eyes half-closed.

"Bye, Grampa," I say. "See you soon."

This time he sits up. "Bye, Mae-mae." His words come slowly but clear. I smile, walk over, and give him a gentle hug. He feels like the same old Grampa. Maybe he's closer to better than I thought.

As we head back to the elevator, Mom says, "You did great. And I haven't seen your smile in days." She nods toward where Jasper sits, his head in his book again. "Who knew you'd make a new friend here of all places?"

8

MOST KIDS GO TO BIRTHDAY PARTIES, SWIMMING pools, or parks on special Saturdays. I go to tablescaping competitions held at various convention centers and county fairgrounds. Rules vary slightly from one competition to the next, but normally there are three divisions: Youth, General, and Expert. Even though any table could win Best in Show, they almost always come from the Expert Division, and they almost always go to one person. That person is not my mom.

Lorna Diamond wears sequined blazers and wins nearly every single time—normally with a perfect score. Mom's only beaten her once in four years, and that was when Lorna had the stomach flu. Not long after her most recent loss to Lorna, Mom bought the book *Winning Isn't Everything*. But I'm pretty sure she hasn't read it yet.

Mom wipes down every inch of her table with pale blue glass cleaner and a microfiber cloth. We both wear these special white gloves. In her first competition she had points deducted for a fingerprint on a knife and has never gotten over it.

We unpack the suitcases, open the boxes, and organize all the supplies on the floor. "Mabel, would you polish the glass marbles again?" Mom swipes a lint roller over all the linens.

Her theme is Frozen Wonderland, and she's made a centerpiece of huge, fake evergreen branches spray-painted silver, coated in glitter, and dotted with pearls, like solid dew drops. They'll be in a vase filled with glass marbles. But what Mom calls her "showstopper" is a small tree that'll sit on the back edge; it's a wide artificial cedar about three feet tall, flocked in a thick blanket of fake snow that looks a little too much like shaving cream. The whole table is peppered with silver pinecones.

Every single item is brand spanking new and looks it.

Mom won't upcycle for her tables. So far, she's passed on a whole crate of vintage milk bottles, a near-perfect pair of jadeite candlesticks, and an antique brass birdcage—all spot-on centerpiece material in my opinion. She says it's because she's scored on the condition of the items, and she can't risk being marked down for wear and tear. But my guess is, it has more to do with Grampa and how much she hates his collections.

Mom takes a deep breath. "With all that's going on with your grampa, it's been hard to keep my head in the game, but I think we really have a chance this time." She points to the bag of marbles and the cloth I'm supposed to be using to clean them. I know "we" doesn't really include me.

"Time for the tables to turn." Mom winks at me.

I help unfold Mom's tablecloth. It's almost sheer but also slightly shiny, like thickly woven spiderwebs. My job is to hold it up while she applies a thick mist of aerosol hair spray to prevent any static cling. By the time she's done, I'm coughing, and my eyes burn. This is going to be a dud day for sure.

"Thank you, hon." Mom carefully takes the corners from me. She's already steamed it twice to get rid of the fold lines.

I scan the room. The theme is Wander in Wonderland. There are four Alice in Wonderland tables, a Disney Wonderland table (complete with a three-foot-tall exact replica of the Disneyland Castle done in papier-mâché), and unfortunately, another Frozen Wonderland table that caused Mom to drop a few words I can't repeat. Not a chipped, worn-in, or worn-out thing in sight.

Mom snaps her fingers and points to the marbles again. She positions a small standing picture frame that holds her fake menu, all courses best served cold. Last year, Tamela Carter broke down in tears when she lost points for including a cheese platter but had no cheese knife as part of her table setting. The thing is, no one actually sits at the tables, much less eats there. Most of the time there aren't even chairs.

All this stuff bought only to be set up, judged, and never used—I don't get why Mom loves it so much. This whole room makes me think about all we don't have in common.

As I rub each identical marble, I think of Grampa. The marbles in his collection are all different, some swirled with colors like ribbon candy, some solid but with tiny air bubbles frozen in the glass. Though I can guarantee not a one has ever been polished, they're all loved. That's what makes collections special, and all this stuff here...not so special.

"Done," I say. "Can I walk around?"

Mom only nods then cranes her head this way and that, staring at the silver branches of her centerpiece like they've done something wrong.

I decide to go check out the other wintry wonderland table. Even from a distance, it's easy to tell the craftmanship is Lorna Diamond's. The glass goblets are encrusted with little rhinestones. Her tablecloth is a thick blanket of batting used to stuff quilts and plush animals but coated with an inch of fake snow; it's all been lightly dusted with fine-grain glitter. And the showstopper is a castle made from clear resin meant to look like ice. But the very middle is empty. That's Lorna's signature move—to wait until the last minute to place her centerpiece. It always draws a crowd.

I look over at Mom, still inspecting her work. She steps back, flaps out her polishing cloth to get rid of any debris, and starts wiping everything down again. The room reeks of Windex and Aqua Net. I'm thinking the plates on Lorna Diamond's table are the same strange blue as the glass cleaner when from behind me someone says, "Your mom looks a little frazzled."

I turn and have to squint. The harsh overhead lighting glares off Lorna Diamond's gold-sequined blazer; it's like staring into the sun.

"Maybe she could use a hand?" Lorna flashes her teeth in a forced smile, then eyeballs her table like she suspects I might have tampered with something. In the Expert Division, participants must follow the American Standard Table Setting Rules, a bunch of detailed guidelines all focused on creating the perfect table. A slightly misplaced dessert spoon? Say goodbye to a ribbon.

"Good luck today," I say with a big smile, then stare hard at her table just to keep her guessing.

Lorna only nods, definitely doesn't wish me and Mom any luck, and then pulls a rolling suitcase up to the edge of her table. Mom makes a point of turning her back, ignoring the crowd slowly building around Lorna. Lorna Diamond also pretends not to notice, but I see her smile as she snaps open the latches and takes out a centerpiece made entirely of glass icicles, all different sizes jutting out here and there, like an icy sunburst. It's beautiful.

The crowd gasps and so do I. Not at the centerpiece, but at what it's resting in. A large pale blue vase with constellation cuts up and down the curved sides. I know that glasswork better than my multiplication facts. It's a vintage Tiara Indiana Glass Constellation Vase in ice blue.

I'm dying to reach out, tilt up the bottom, and see if the TJ is there like the signature on the bottom of my Amberina basket. That's not some meaningless brand-new vase. I'd bet my whole collection that it's a heart find.

When I turn around, Mom has quit pretending not to watch. Her eyes tell me she's thinking the same thing as me—she's already lost.

83

The ride back home is long and quiet. Every time I think about meeting Jasper tomorrow, my heartbeat speeds up. Mom must feel the exact opposite.

She won second place. To Mom, second isn't perfect, but it's so close that it's worse than third. Lorna Diamond winning with practically the same idea must make this loss sting even more than the others. I should say something, but I can't think of anything helpful.

She has me, so at least she isn't ice-olated.

Losing is snow laughing matter.

But now isn't the time for a walk through winter punderland.

Mom pulls into a parking spot in our apartment complex, stops the car, but doesn't get out. She touches her pearls and looks up to the second floor where the curtains she sewed block the view into our living room. "I was distracted today, but I've got to do better than second if I want to change things for us." She gives me a sad smile. "Another second-place win means I'm less likely to qualify for the National Expo. Winning there would be a life changer."

I want to tell her that until a week ago I was

perfectly happy with my life, but I can't say that. And I absolutely can't tell her my plan. She'd say no again without giving it a single thought, just like she does to my ideas for more interesting tables.

So, I just sit there until Mom opens her door with a sigh and walks off without looking back to see if I follow.

9

MOM SPENDS SUNDAY MORNING PREPPING FOR A late-afternoon wedding. By the time we get to Whispering Pines it's almost noon. Mom and I walk around the second floor with two Boston cream donuts and two egg-white-and-spinach breakfast wraps. The donuts are for Grampa. The wraps are for me and Mom. Guess who placed the order? Not me.

The cafeteria is mostly empty. Mom checks her phone. "We're not going to be able to stay long. I'll go get Grampa. Want to wait here?"

I nod and as soon as she's out of sight the same woman I noticed during our first visit walks over.

She's wearing a sweat suit with gold-striped Adidas sneakers again.

She waves as she approaches. "You must be Robert's granddaughter. Same beautiful brown eyes."

I smile and say, "Thanks."

"Tell him Antonia says hello." She walks by me toward a group of residents gathered in the hallway.

A minute later, Mom pulls up with Grampa in his wheelchair. And before she can sit down, Grampa grabs one of the wraps, gives me a very slow wink, and takes a big bite.

Mom frowns. "Dad, that was for Mabel."

"Guess she'll have to eat the donuts." Grampa's speech is still a little slurred, and even though I know it hasn't been long, I keep hoping that I'll visit and he'll be walking and talking like his old self. The cry-knot is suddenly back, and I don't think even donuts are going to make me feel any better.

Grampa puts one of his big hands on my back and gives me two solid pats. "Eat before I change my mind." His voice is the same though, so familiar that I'm able to squeeze a real smile out after all.

"Oh, that lady who wears the Adidas shoes told

me to tell you hi. But I forgot her name already." I bite into the Boston cream and realize I was wrong—donuts do make things better.

"That's Toni," Grampa says.

Mom gives Grampa a sly smile. "Seems like you're settling into your new community nicely," she says.

Grampa nods. "It's not too bad."

I whip my head around to face him. How could he say that? Of course it's bad. It's the worst. The duddiest of duds.

As much as I want Grampa to be happy, he already has a community, and it isn't here. It's with me.

Mom gives Grampa a play-by-play of her table-scaping win. "Getting into the Expo would be a dream come true," Mom says. "But I'll be up against some of the top tablescaping artists in the country."

Grampa looks at me and raises his eyebrows. Mom sees it and her smile vanishes. "What I do takes a lot of creativity and a ton of work and planning, but I get that it's not the same as *collecting*."

"Janie, I think your tables are beautiful." There are long pauses between Grampa's words. It's hard for me to hear him sound so changed, but it must be harder for him. I stare at Mom, hoping she'll let it go and give Grampa a break for once.

She just mumbles, "That's why you've only gone to one competition."

Mom cleans the table, snatching up the bags and napkins. When she gets up to toss our trash, Grampa stops her by putting his hand on hers. "It's okay," she says. "I've got to get a move on. There's still more to do to get this wedding off and running before this afternoon."

While she's at the bins, Grampa looks over at me and shrugs.

I stare at Mom's back. For a split second, I wonder what it was like for Mom to have Grampa for a dad. Maybe she felt like she never really had his complete attention, like he never really saw her. Maybe she felt like I do sometimes about her.

Mom and I both give Grampa a hug, but when Mom reaches toward his wheelchair, he shakes his head. "I can do it."

"You sure?" Mom asks.

Grampa does a long, single nod. "It's good for me."

He rolls backward and says, "Love you, Mae-mae." I give him one more hug. He doesn't say anything to Mom.

She turns to me. "You want me to call Mrs. Hammons and see if she'll come hang out with you again?"

"Please don't," I say. Mom laughs, and we walk out together. I take one more look back. Grampa is stopped and watching us leave. He lifts his hand to wave. I wave back just before the elevator closes.

·~ato~·

When Mom works an afternoon wedding, she leaves after lunch and gets home late in the evening.

"Are you sure you'll be okay?" she asks.

"I'm sure." I've stayed home alone before but not for hours on end. Normally I go to Grampa's house.

"Well, you have your phone. If you need anything, you text me or call Mrs. Hammons if it can't wait."

I nod.

Mom pulls out and waves while I stand in the parking lot and wave back. We're both acting different after what happened with Grampa.

Back inside the apartment, I pace for ten minutes across our small living room when I get a text from Jasper. Are we cleared for duty? I think of Grampa sitting there in his wheelchair as the elevator closed. I text back: Meet me at the strip mall at 12th and E. Robinson at 5:30.

I've got plenty of time to bike to Grampa's and figure out a way to attach the wagon. I close the front door as quietly as possible, use the back staircase just in case Mrs. Hammons decides to look out her window, and race to my bike.

It's almost a twenty-minute ride to Grampa's. I breeze past Homeland and then take Hinkle Drive until I see the still-in-bloom crepe myrtle trees that line the streets of Grampa's neighborhood. At the sight of his overgrown lawn, I think of the last time I was there with him and tell myself there'll be a next time soon.

Grampa always leaves the shed unlocked. Inside it looks sort of like a tiny hardware store. The shelves are all stocked and organized. Our wagon sits, filled with the milk crates we take on expeditions, plus our gloves, hand sanitizer, and headlamps. The grabbing tools rest against the wall. I leave the headlamps and take everything else.

Using one of Grampa's short bungee cords, I secure the handle of the wagon to the rear rack. The basket in the front, the bell, the brown leather seat, and even the handlebars are all upgrades from my and Grampa's finds. Mom says my bike looks like a patchwork quilt, but I like it just the way it is.

After a few test runs on the driveway, I decide it'll do. I'll have to take corners slow, but it works. I use three releasable cable ties to attach the grabbing tool to the side of the wagon, and I'm all set with half an hour to spare, plenty of time to water our garden and Grampa's plants.

Grampa's backyard is one of my favorite places. His planters aren't pots; they're rainboots, colanders, even old cinderblocks. The dirt in our little garden is dry and cracked and the green shoots are drooping. I laugh when I see the beets, but the laugh catches and turns into almost crying.

I hang my head and notice a streak of bright green across the dry grass. Our hummingbird feeders hang from a nearby pine tree. We made them from two green glass Sprite bottles. Just a few weeks ago we sat and watched a tiny hummingbird hover and drink sugar water. Grampa looked over at me, smiled, and said, "Sometimes the best things in life are right in your own backyard."

The lawn chairs still sit in the same spot they were that day. I look over at them and take a deep breath. This is where Grampa belongs, and I'm going to get him back home no matter what it takes.

After watering everything, I let a slow scan of Grampa's yard, filled with treasures, soothe my heart before I put away the hose, buckle my bike helmet, and take off up Windsor Drive toward the strip mall.

Jasper is waiting in front of the Burger Brothers. He doesn't see me at first because he's reading a book again, balancing his bike between his legs.

He looks up as I pull to a stop. "Hey, Mabel." His face breaks open in a smile. It's a really nice smile.

"Hey, you ready?" I ask.

Jasper nods and slides his book into his backpack. "Follow me," I say, and bike across the parking lot. When Mom and I drove by, I hadn't noticed what kind of store it was, but now I stop and read the sign: BABY OF MINE.

Jasper pulls up beside me. "What's wrong?"

"Nothing. It's just electronics would be way better. Frank won't take baby clothes."

"We can't give up yet. The heroes always run into what seem like insurmountable obstacles right in the beginning. And who's Frank?"

"He owns the pawn shop and he's not interested in clothes—his or other people's."

"What about those stores that resell clothes, and the owner gets a percentage?" Jasper asks.

"Consignment." I nod. "Not a bad idea." But I need more than a percentage. "I'll figure it out."

Jasper puts one foot on a pedal. "Lead the way."

We circle around the back of the mall, where all the dumpsters are. Sometimes they're locked, but the one behind Baby of Mine is open. I scan the area looking for any signs marking it as private property, just as a man walks out and throws a garbage bag in. He closes the dumpster and wipes his hands on his jeans.

"Perfect timing," I whisper. "Let's bike around a little and give him time to clear out."

Jasper nods and we head back to the mostly empty parking lot, making wide circles. Every time I look back at Jasper, he gives me that huge smile of his. It's impossible not to smile back. Finally, we see the same man leaving in a beat-up brown truck.

We take off in a race and skid to a stop right in front of the dumpster. "My Grampa always says the best things are unexpected, and that's what makes treasure hunting special—you never know what you'll find."

Jasper nods and we just sit there for a minute. Grampa and I love this moment before we start. Anything seems possible. "Once a woman found a painting in a dumpster. Turned out to be a famous etching done by a Chinese artist and sold for almost sixteen thousand dollars at auction." This fact is courtesy of my and Grampa's favorite show, *Collector's Menagerie*.

"Whoa." Jasper adjusts his glasses.

"Ready?" I prop up my bike.

"And so it begins," Jasper whispers.

I laugh and shake my head. "You're different."

Jasper's big smile fades a little. "In a good way," I add. I unwrap the bungee cord and roll the wagon over to the dumpster. "Here. Grab a pair of gloves. Then take a milk crate and turn it over to use like a step stool."

It takes both of us to lift the lid.

"So, I'll go through the bags, but I need you to keep a lookout. If you see someone drive by and slow down or get out their phone, we should probably head out."

Jasper's smile disappears. "This isn't illegal, is it?"

"No. But some people seem to think it should be. So, they'll call the police. Normally, if the cops even come, they just ask us not to leave a mess. Worst case, they'll ask us to move along. But as long as nothing is marked 'Private Property' we're okay. But it's up to you. If you're worried about getting in trouble and want to go, I'd understand."

Grampa only considers one place off-limits—the Merkle Creek Mall. He won't say what happened there, but he does say that trash-to-cash hunts should be done rarely, carefully, and under cover of night.

Jasper shrugs. "Might as well. Nothing else to do in this podunk town."

Abner is the third largest city in all of Oklahoma, but I decide to keep that fact to myself. A lookout and an extra pair of hands would be nice, but they're not essential. I get to work and pull the first bag out with ease and rest it on the ground.

Jasper comes over and watches as I open the ties on top. It's full of stuffed animals, varied in color and size. But they're all pigs. Every last one. We crouch there for a minute and stare.

"That's just sad," Jasper finally says. We both look into the bag, then at each other, and laugh. We laugh until we're almost falling over.

I point to one. "That one's *hogging* all the space."

Jasper nods to another. "This one's *boared*."

"Look. His *pigmentation* is off." I bite my lip, waiting for Jasper to beat that one.

He's quiet, thinking for a minute, before he singles out a different plush pig and says, "And him, he looks pretty *disgruntled*."

"Nice," I say. "That reminds me, I don't know your last name."

Jasper snorts. "How do pigs remind you of that?"

"Because mine is Cunningham. I can't hear my last

name without thinking of a pig in a detective outfit. Cunning ham. Crafty pig. Shrewd sow. Sneaky swine."

"You are different in a good way too." Jasper shakes his head and laughs again. "It's Ketchum."

I nod and think for a second. "Jasper's great, if you can Ketchum."

Jasper just looks at me. "That was terrible," he says, but his big smile is all the way back.

I smile too. "Enough chatting. Eyes on the road."

He salutes and turns to face the back alley.

After about half an hour we've got the wagon loaded with baby clothes, stuffed animals, a few fancy night-lights, and even a brand-new bouncer. As I secure everything with the extra bungee cords and reattach the wagon to my bike, Jasper says, "I've got to get home. If I'm not back by dinner, Mom'll freak."

"Where'd you tell her you were going?" I ask.

"Library." He motions to his backpack full of books. "And it wasn't a complete lie."

"See you on the bus tomorrow," I say. "And thanks for coming."

"No problem." He starts to pedal off and stops.

"Can we do this again? It was the most fun I've had in the last few months."

"Sure." I wave and want to ask him why he came to begin with, but I still have to stop by Grampa's on my way home and store our haul, all before Mom gets back. I watch him as he pedals off. He's right about one thing. It was fun, definitely not a dud day.

10

MONDAY MORNING, MOM WAVES A PIECE OF PAPER to get my attention. It's one of her lists. She loves lists.

"Got any ideas for stuff Grampa might need? I'm going to pick up a few things, and then we can visit him together this afternoon."

"What about his marble collection or the record player and his records?" I ask. Mom nods but I notice she doesn't add them to her list.

"So, listen," she says. "I was down over my second-place win, but that red satin ribbon gave me an idea. What about a red bandanna-print tablecloth?

The theme at the Expo this year is Classic Americana, so I've been thinking country all along, but now I'm leaning toward a more farm-to-table inspiration. Keep it simple. What do you think?"

I think I don't know what she's talking about, but I mumble, "Mm-hmm," and shove the last bite of toast in my mouth. She's forgotten all about Grampa and her list. How can she go on and on about her tables with his whole life falling apart right in front of her?

Mom sighs. "I know I might not make it in, and it's over a month away, but if I prepare for the best, the best just might come my way."

I back toward the door and try to smile. "Sounds like a plan."

Mom waves the paper again, this time as a goodbye.

The first day I was back at school after Grampa's stroke, Ashley gave me a hug and said she was sorry and hoped Grampa was okay. Even Farrah said she was sorry, though she never even met Grampa and knows negative one thousand about the situation.

But now they're back to pretty much ignoring me and I'm pretending not to notice.

I'm a little late this morning, and by the time I get there, everyone else is already on the bus. I climb the steps and look down the aisle. Farrah is sitting in the fourth row on the left side by the window. My seat.

Ashley glances up at me from her normal spot. I sit in the fourth row on the right, aisle side, and it feels weird, like I'm wearing my jeans backward.

I look at Ashley, and she looks at me. Then I notice that she and Farrah have on makeup. First the matching outfits and now this. Suddenly, it feels like I'm wearing my jeans backward *and* they just shrunk three sizes.

"Did your mom have a competition this weekend?" she asks.

"What kind of competition, like a beauty pageant for moms," Farrah says, and giggles. How does she know my mom used to be a beauty queen? Ashley won't meet my eye.

I ignore Farrah and ask, "What's on your face?"

"Blush, eye shadow, eyeliner, *and* mascara. Farrah

showed me how to do it this weekend. Then we watched some YouTube tutorials. The eyeliner was sort of tricky. You like it?" They have the exact same shade smeared across their eyelids.

Even though I know I need to fix our friendship, my jealous feelings sneak out. "Not really. Your eyelashes kind of look like spider legs." I actually think she looks good, sort of like a lemur, but a pretty lemur.

Farrah laughs. "You did get it on a little thick, Ash," she says.

Ash? Ashley hates that nickname. And I hate that Farrah agreed with me, but I can't take it back.

Ashley's neck flushes with red splotches the way it does when she's upset. I'm guessing she's not upset about the nickname. More than anything I want to tell Farrah to get out of my seat. If I was sitting next to Ashley I could apologize, but the aisle between us feels too wide to say anything over. So I just stare straight ahead and think of all the puns I want to say but can't.

Sorry I lashed out.

I owe you an eyeballogy.

But it's not my fault your mascara is mascary.

The Ashley from this summer would shake her head at my bad jokes, then she'd bump my shoulder with hers, and we'd laugh together.

McKenna Higginbotham sits in front of me. She turns around and smiles. "Hey, Mabel." I make myself smile back. We've never been friends really, but in second grade she did an experiment with two balloons, proving that air has mass. And I've always loved her last name. She has five different-colored hairbands, and her ponytail swings and bounces as the bus takes off.

Jasper gets on at Bolivar Street and waves as soon as he meets my eye. He high-fives McKenna, sits by her, then turns around to talk to me. "I'm in science club with McKenna. Meets every Wednesday after school." He glances over toward my old seat. "You could join if you want. It's something to do."

"Maybe," I say. It feels good to have him include me, but once we take off, some of the places Grampa and I go together flash by. Trying to push down thoughts of him seems to make them stronger. I look over at Ashley and she turns her back to me. Jasper and McKenna talk about the upcoming science fair. By the time the school is in view, I already wish the day were over.

So far, I haven't managed to fix a single thing, not Grampa's situation and not my friendship with Ashley. I've got a whole wagon full of baby stuff sure *not* to make me much cash, if I can resell it at all. It'll take time to raise money for Grampa's expenses, but Ashley seems to like me less and less by the minute. Treasure hunting takes patience and perseverance; maybe friendships do too?

When we get to class, Ashley slams her notebook on her desk. I get mine out too, the sorry I need to say about her makeup still stuck in my mouth. Suddenly all my feelings about Grampa and Ashley are mixing up together. I clench my pencil and try Mom's strategy and remember I'm grateful that Grampa will be okay.

Mrs. Kirkpatrick lets everyone settle and says, "Over these next few weeks we'll be studying energy, forces, and motion. To celebrate all we've learned we'll do a fun project as an end-of-unit assessment rather than a test."

Some kids cheer. One boy even stands and does a little dance.

Mrs. Kirkpatrick starts up the SMART Board and shows us a drawing of what looks like a comic strip—a man with a bushy mustache is eating soup with a contraption on his head, his spoon activating a lever that throws a cracker to a bird, who somehow fills a bucket, tripping an alarm that fires a rocket, setting in motion a windshield wiper holding a napkin to wipe the man's mustache. It's ridiculous and hilarious, like an illustration of a really bad joke; Grampa would love it.

"Does anyone know what this is?" Mrs. Kirkpatrick asks.

Behind me McKenna is practically hopping in her seat until Mrs. Kirkpatrick calls on her. "It's a Rube Goldberg machine, a machine built to perform a simple task in an overly complicated way."

"That's right. So, you'll be designing your own chain-reaction machine using two of the simple machines that we'll study over the course of the unit, and at least three energy transfers. We'll do most of the planning in class, but you'll need to bring in your items to build a mock-up with your partner and prepare for your in-class presentation. Turn to someone next to you, and now you're a team of two."

Ashley stares straight ahead. So, I turn around to the desk behind me and say, "Hey, McKenna, would you want to team up with me?"

If McKenna's surprised, she doesn't show it. "Sure. I've got a lot of ideas I'd like to run by you."

The shock on Ashley's face makes me almost regret not asking her. It would've been a way to spend time together, but while I sit there and listen to McKenna, I remember the details. I remember the Shop-n-Save, how Ashley sat on the bus, sat right beside me and didn't say a word. I remember how she shifted in her seat and wouldn't meet my eye. I remember that day in the parking lot of the Tuesday Thrift, when David called Grampa the Junkman, and she pretended not to recognize me.

I look over at her, and she glares at me. I glare right back. Her face shifts from angry to confused. The fact that she has no idea what she's done and it's impossible to explain makes me even angrier.

11

I GRAB A BAG LUNCH FROM THE CAFETERIA AND go to the library to avoid sitting with Ashley and Farrah. After lunch we have conference period, where we're allowed to go to any teacher's office hour and ask questions. I decide to stay in the library and crunch some numbers. Mom always says be useful today and you'll be thankful tomorrow.

If Grampa needs an extra two hundred dollars a month, that's two thousand four hundred dollars for the year. That sounds like a lot, but really, I'm just one big find away from success. But it's going to take more than a bunch of stuffed pigs.

All through the rest of my classes, I try to think where and when Jasper and I might hunt again. At the final bell I rush to the bus so Farrah can't get to my seat first. Ashley will have to sit by me. I can apologize, and then I bet she'll apologize too.

A man across the street is watering his yard, and while I wait, I remember the last time I was with Ashley and things felt normal. It was the weekend before she left for camp. Mr. Ruse runs the sprinklers on the large front lawn of my apartment complex every Friday. We ran through the spray, weaving in and out trying to avoid being hit but also screaming with joy whenever we were.

We collapsed next to each other, our hair soaked and plastered flat with blades of grass stuck to our legs. She hit her bare foot into mine. "Ever play airplane?" she asked. I shook my head. "Come on, stand up and reach out for my hands." I did like she said. She rested her feet against my stomach, and I leaned over and took her hands in mine. "Now, push off and I'll lift you up."

I pushed off and her feet pressed into my stomach as she struggled to balance me above her. It only lasted a few seconds, and then I fell and landed with a thud on one of her legs. Ashley let out her wild, snorting cackle. We laughed until my stomach hurt. She'd sighed and said, "My dad used to do that all the time." I should've asked her if she wanted to talk about it, said I was sorry about her parents' divorce, anything. But I'd just bumped her foot with mine. I wonder if that's when she decided to let me go.

When Ashley gets on, she doesn't say a word, barely looks my way, and sits across the aisle. As the bus roars to life, she and Farrah already have their heads together, whispering and giggling, and completely ignoring me.

I take out my assignment from language arts and pretend to read. One thing keeps running through my mind: *Today is Monday, and Monday is* Collector's Menagerie. But then thinking of my and Grampa's favorite show just makes me feel worse.

I walk off the bus feeling like I've lost one more thing I used to look forward to, when Farrah says, "Bye, Mabel." Something about the way she says it makes it clear that she isn't being nice.

McKenna jogs a few steps to catch up with me. She glances back at Farrah. "Believe it or not, Farrah and I used to be friends in first grade. My mom says people can be disappointing, but they can be surprising too."

I swallow hard and nod. Then she walks beside me for half the block. "You should come over sometime."

"Yeah. Sounds fun," I say. We part at the corner. But over the few blocks to my house, I start to wonder if it really would be fun.

Maybe friendships work like a favorite book. The first time I read *Hide and Seek* by Kate Messner, I didn't know it'd be my favorite book right from the very first page. I watch McKenna round the corner and head to her house and wonder if Jasper, McKenna, and I are just on the first page.

Does making new friends mean I'm giving up on Ashley? Everything's so mixed up that I don't know what I think anymore. Not to mention, I've only focused on making trash-to-cash finds lately, which is about as far away from heart finds as I can get.

By the time I walk into my apartment, I'm not even sure how I feel about watching *Collector's Menagerie*. It doesn't make sense, but suddenly I'm mad at Grampa. Why'd he have to be scavenging right on my bus route? Why'd he go for that Fall Cleanup haul without me? If he was here, I'd be okay, everything would be okay.

I walk in and toss my backpack roughly on the floor. Mom's at the dining table with papers scattered in front of her. She's taken the day off to sort things out for Grampa, and I can tell by the way she's holding her head up with her hand that she's on the phone with his insurance again. Her phone is squeezed between her ear and her shoulder, and she holds a pencil frozen above a notebook. She's all scrunched, her body and her face.

"Use speakerphone and just set it on the table," I snap.

She whispers, "Old habit." But maybe she doesn't want me to hear what's being said.

"Okay. Well, I'll just have to call back... again." Then she puts the phone down and says, "It's impossible to get a straight answer, but it seems like once Grampa is discharged from Whispering Pines, he's responsible for twenty percent of all his out-patient care. But that's for me to worry about." She shakes her head then looks up at me. "How was school?"

I think about all the bad maybes Mom must be dealing with, and I say, "Great. Really great."

Mom smiles. "Well, I'm glad one of us had a good day." I grab my bag and take off toward my room. "Just a sec," she says. "I was thinking you could let me visit with Grampa on my own this afternoon to talk through some of this financial stuff with him."

"I do have a lot of homework," I say.

"But I could come by and get you when we're done talking and we could all have dinner together?"

"I'll just stay home if that's okay. I need a break from Whispering Pines."

She puts her pencil down. I know that look. It's the one she gives her tables when they don't turn out exactly like she wants. "Whispering Pines is a really great place. Grampa's getting settled in. He'll start meeting with an occupational therapist soon and get counseling too."

I suspect Whispering Pines is probably as great as my recent bus rides. And Grampa's only been there a week. How settled in could he be? These are things I might normally say, but today I figure both Mom and I are feeling pretty scrunched, so I just nod.

"Still don't want to go?" she asks.

"School comes first, right?" I hold my hands up like there's nothing to be done.

Mom gives me a look like she's also not saying a lot she normally would. "So, you'll be able to go tomorrow then."

I nod and start down the hall to my room. "Sure."

Mom gets up, follows me, and stands in my doorway. "Guess what?" she asks.

"What?" Suddenly, all these good maybes flood my mind. Maybe Grampa's fully recovered. Maybe she's found a way not to sell his house. Maybe we'll all move in together.

"My application to participate in the Sooner State Regional Tablescaping Competition was accepted. The theme is A Night in Paradise. Winners who placed in at least three state-level competitions gain automatic entrance into the National Expo. And here's the kicker: The winner of Best of Show at the Expo gets a spot as a competitor on a new Hearth & Home Network program called *Top Table* hosted by none other than Arletta Paisley! It's a little like those baking competition shows, only you're judged on your table designs."

"Sounds good, Mom."

Her face falls even further. "Crafting mogul and television star Arletta Paisley?"

"Cool," I say, but it must sound like I don't mean it because Mom sighs and closes my door.

I take out my math book, leave it on my bed, and instead pick up my Amberina basket. There is a nick in the handle, and the smooth chipped spot fits the tip of my pinky finger perfectly.

Grampa and I found my basket two summers ago. Archie greeted us with hugs and butterscotch hard candies like always. Then Grampa and I headed for the aisles. And there it was, casting sunset colors on the speckled linoleum.

I lifted it off the shelf and turned it in the sun,

watching the colors change on the floor, then looked for an artist's mark on the bottom, because that's what serious glassware collectors do. I traced my finger over the raised T and J.

"Forty-nine ninety-nine on eBay," Grampa whispered, checking his phone.

On the handle a sticker marked $2.50 took our breath away. This is what Grampa calls a steal, though it doesn't involve actual theft.

But then I noticed the chip. "It's messed up."

"No, it's one of a kind. You won't find another exactly like it anywhere else in the world." Then Grampa looked straight at me. "What some might think of as imperfection is what makes antiques unique—special because of all their variations, just like people." Then he nudged me with his shoulder, letting me know that he wasn't only talking about the basket.

I've been collecting antique glass baskets ever since. But my Amberina one is my favorite. Sticking my finger in the chipped spot reminds me that Grampa was talking about me, that he thinks I'm special just the way I am. With Grampa, that's where I fit perfectly.

I turn the little basket around in the late afternoon light before resting it back on my windowsill. It's my first heart find and just looking at it makes me feel better. Getting Grampa home is my top priority—that's what my heart needs most.

My homework takes longer than usual. When Mom knocks on my door, I've only finished one of the reading responses I'm supposed to do.

"I'm about to head out. You sure you don't want me to swing by and get you later? I don't mind."

"I'm sure," I say.

"I'll pick you up some dinner on the way home." Mom walks out without giving me a hug or kissing the top of my head.

Ten minutes before seven o'clock and Mom still isn't home. I pace in front of the TV. On the bar that separates our small dining room from our even smaller kitchen, she's left one of her self-help books. *Get Over Yourself* is the title, and three sticky notes poke out for me. She does this often, and I think it's her way of trying to get me to improve myself. But it doesn't feel very helpful.

I open the book and she's highlighted the lines "We often serve as the biggest obstacles to our own happiness. Have the courage to get out of your own way." I roll my eyes clear to the ceiling and don't bother looking at the other two sticky notes.

At five till, Mom texts that she'll be home in half an hour, and she'll pick up tacos. Maybe she knew about my and Grampa's Monday-night meals after all.

I sit on the couch, pick up the remote, and turn on the TV.

Collector's Menagerie travels the country appraising everyday, regular people's antiques. There's a staff of appraisers, all with specialties. Anyone can apply for tickets, and then they get to bring in their most prized possession to find out what it's really worth.

The episode opens with the camera panning a crowd of people ambling through a convention center. There's the comfortable chatter of a whole lot of people in one space, like the noise in the Icon during the dinner rush. I watch as they cut to a woman introduced to the audience as Edna Worn.

Some people make it on camera because they paid next to nothing for an item that's worth a whole lot. But sometimes it's because they paid a ton for a fake; those are hard to watch. Each episode usually contains two really amazing finds or fails; they kick the episode off with one before the title sequence and then end with the other before running the closing credits.

Edna has wild, white curls and a shirt with more ruffles than a petticoat. I sort through all the possible puns a name like Worn offers. Edna's brought in a tiny table, and across from her is Grampa's favorite appraiser, Ray Reno. Ray has a raspy voice and a soft spot for American folk art. He once teared up over a wall-pocket sculpture made entirely of pinecones.

"How'd you come to own this beauty?" Ray asks.

"My sister picked it up at an estate sale in 1972 for about fifty dollars." Edna pulls at one of the ruffles on her collar, but she looks at the table with such warmth that I'm almost sure it's speaking to her heart in that very moment.

"Well, would you believe that this little fellow dates back not to the 1970s but the 1770s?" Ray asks.

This is when Grampa and I would normally scoot to the edge of the couch, because a table that old is bound to be worth a lot even if it's been dipped in bubblegum. But I don't scoot. This time I watch Edna's face brighten as she's filled with all kinds of good maybes.

"This is a Philadelphia candlestand. And a very similar table sits in the Brooklyn Museum." Ray squats and gently releases a hinge on the tabletop, so that half of it falls and rests flush with the stand. "It's solid mahogany," he goes on, "and were it in its original condition, I'd say it'd be worth close to one hundred thousand dollars."

And here's the problem; that table is nowhere near its original condition. Edna has painted every inch of it a very bright purple.

"With professional restoration, you could regain

quite a bit of value, and as is, it's still worth close to eight thousand. Possibly more to a collector," Ray says in a reassuring tone. "The issue is often these older items have been so changed that they can't truly be brought back to what they once were. And it's the original patina that a collector is after."

I can't take my eyes off Edna. There's a change in her face as the difference between one hundred thousand and eight thousand sinks in. But it's more than that. It's not sadness or anger. It's loss.

The show's music starts up, signaling the beginning of a commercial break—all instruments, happy jazz, but old-fashioned. Honestly, it's a dorky theme song. And I remember Grampa doing a silly knock-kneed dance in front of his TV while holding a taco and spilling shredded cheese like confetti. I remember laughing and feeling embarrassed at the same time. I remember how with Grampa I don't have to struggle to fit in, together we just *are*.

I've always believed that he and I could fix anything. It never occurred to me that he might not be there to.

Before I know it, I'm crying so hard that I don't hear Mom come in. She sits, grabs the remote, and turns off the TV, then wraps both arms around me.

"Oh, Mabel," she says. "It will get better. He will get better." But her voice is choked up by tears and the opposite of convincing.

12

MOM STANDS IN FRONT OF ME WITH HER HANDS on her hips. "I'm going to see Grampa today and you're coming with me. Enough sulking. Getting back on our feet is the only way to take the first steps forward." It's been three days and I've come up with one excuse after another for not going to Whispering Pines, and each day that passes I feel worse about it.

She walks into the kitchen to pour another cup of coffee. "Oh, I almost forgot to tell you. That show you and Grampa love? It's going to be at the Expo this year, same convention center, same weekend. Since the grand prize for the Expo is a spot on *Top*

Table, and *Collector's Menagerie* is on the same net-work, they're using it as a promotional opportunity."

"Really?" I ask. Grampa and I have always talked about going together, and for a minute the idea makes me forget everything that's wrong.

"I'm taking it as a good sign, like Grampa will be there with me. That is, if I get in." Mom smiles at me, then blows on her steaming coffee. The National Expo is the biggest stage there is for tablescapers. A win like that might make Mom explode. Or implode, because that'd be less mess and that's more her style. Plus, a chance to be on TV. Mom is smiling to her-self, maybe imagining her first close-up.

The ache in my throat comes back in full force and faster than usual. Suddenly, I feel like screaming that Grampa won't be there with her at all, or with me. And fixing that is what we should be focused on, not her tables.

"So last night after you went to bed, I applied for tickets. I figured you and I could go whether I get into the Expo or not. Maybe you could take one of your glass baskets?"

Collector's Menagerie is my and Grampa's thing. I

stare at her and then sigh. How can she think I'd go without him?

Mom frowns. "I thought you'd be more excited."

"I'm just tired." I wipe the sleep from my eyes as evidence. I can't tell her what I really think. Besides, it's not like Grampa could go, not now.

Since Mom has the morning off, she drives me to school. Before I get out, she leans over and kisses my forehead. "Think positive. We are strong, we are brave, and we will get through this. New challenges are often new opportunities," she whispers. I'm not sure if she's talking to me or herself.

When I get to Mrs. Kirkpatrick's room, Ashley is already sitting at her desk. We haven't spoken to each other much this week, and I've spent every lunch in the library. When I walk by, she doesn't look at me or say good morning or anything at all.

The date on the board reminds me that it's the end of September already. Ashley and I have always come up with costumes for Halloween early so we have plenty of time to work on our outfits. We've been salt and pepper shakers, Frog and Toad, and Peter Pan and Tinkerbell. I found the perfect pair of wings for her at the Tuesday Thrift; she still has them on the back of her desk chair in her room, at least she used to. Last year, we were Anne Shirley and Diana Barry. Mom even taught us to sew a seam, and we worked on the dresses together.

Anne of Green Gables is Ashley's favorite book. She read it and then so did I, and we'd reenact scenes at the playground. We'd taken a solemn oath to be best friends forever, just like in the book. I think of Anne and how she'd never let Diana end their friendship. And I think about how if something isn't working properly it shouldn't just be thrown away. Everything deserves a chance to be salvaged.

"Hi," I say.

Ashley doesn't smile. I don't either.

"Hi," she says back.

Last year, she'd call almost every evening even though we'd just seen each other that day at school. And we'd talk and talk about nothing. Mom would laugh and say, "What else can you two possibly have to say?" Now, I can't think of anything other than hi. Actually, that's not true. I have questions. Like why doesn't she like me as much anymore? What did I do wrong? How could she really like Farrah? I can't ask any of that.

But "hi" is a start.

That's thinking positive.

I spend most of the morning keeping my thoughts from turning negative. It's hard work. When we have free time, I decide to use one of the class computers to see what I missed on *Collector's Menagerie*. That'll give me something to talk to Grampa about tonight. There're no surprises until I scroll down to the "Appraiser's Showcase." A little wooden horse carved by Peter Brubacher appraised for twenty-two thousand dollars.

A wooden carving for twenty-two thousand dollars!

At first, that little bit of information feels like a gift. But by lunchtime I wonder if I should tell Grampa or not. Maybe it'll make him sadder to know he missed our favorite show together. Maybe it'll remind him of how things used to be. Maybe it'll make him worry that nothing will be the same again, and that the things that once made us happy now make us sad.

I go to the line for school lunch and look for Ashley to line up with me like she used to. Kids file past me, finding their friends in line. And then I see her holding a new pink lunch box. She walks right past the line, passes me, and heads toward our table, where Farrah already sits. She waves, so there's that at least.

I get my tray. It's vegetable soup day. I hate vegetable soup day.

Farrah starts talking to me before I can set my tray down. "Hey, Mae. So, Ash and I are thinking of dressing as characters from this show called *Rock-Starz* for the Fall Festival."

Hearing half of Grampa's nickname for me come out of Farah's mouth makes me freeze. Plus, they've planned Halloween costumes without me, and I have no idea what show she's talking about. I've spent lunch in the library for a few days, and now they've ruined something else. Thinking positive is impossible.

I look at Ashley, and she just smiles and says, "It's this group of kids in a band and they're all named after stars."

"I'm going as Vega. Maybe you could be...I don't know. What about Rigel? She's the serious one." The way Farrah says "serious" shows she really means boring.

"I'm going as Polaris. She has blue hair," Ashley says, then looks at me and shrugs, like she can tell I'm disappointed but, oh well, things change. "I think you'd like it. There's even lots of puns. Like they're called the Neptunes. And they say 'Let's rock-et' before they play. Get it?"

Oh, I get it. While I've been missing my favorite show with Grampa, these two have found their own favorite thing to share.

I feel like saying:

Are you Sirius?

That sounds universally ridiculous.

And this sucks like a black hole.

Okay, that last one isn't really a pun and uses a word I'm not supposed to say, but it's accurate.

I feel like saying lots of other things to Ashley that don't involve puns but do involve a whole lot of bad words. Instead I nod, choke down a bit of vegetable soup, and say, "Sure."

I look over and see Jasper sitting at table 4 with McKenna and some other kids. He waves and I wave back. Farrah whips her head around. "How do you know the new kid?"

"His mom is my grampa's speech therapist," I say.

"So, you're like friends with him?" Farrah asks.

"Like 'good friends'?" Ashley adds. Farrah cracks up.

I say, "Just regular friends."

"Sure," Farrah says, and they both laugh this time. "I heard he's from Chicago." She says this like it's a big deal. I struggle to get down another mouthful of lukewarm soup and don't look toward Jasper's table again.

When lunch is over I go to the library for our free conference period. McKenna and I are supposed to meet and work out a plan for our Rube Goldberg machine. We have to draw a design, list out the items we think we'll need, and then Mrs. Kirkpatrick has to approve it.

I decide to look and see if I can find a book on chain-reaction machines, and while I'm wandering the nonfiction aisle, Farrah and Ashley come in and sit at a round table by the magazines. Lunch was awkward, but I decide to step out and wave when I overhear Farrah.

"I'm sorry but does she *really* dig through the trash with her grampa?" Farrah asks, and then laughs. Ashley laughs too. Not her wild, snorty laugh, but a new fake, controlled one. I hate it. But what I hate more is that I hope since she didn't use her real laugh that maybe she doesn't mean it.

When I walk out of the row, I hold my head high and go toward a table across the room. Thankfully, McKenna walks in with Jasper as soon as I sit.

Jasper smiles. "I have the same assignment from Mrs. Kirkpatrick, third period."

McKenna is already making a list. "We need things like train tracks, or tubing. Sometimes the whole machine is mounted on plywood or pegboard or inside a sturdy box. An iron—something that produces heat might be cool."

"My grampa has some of that stuff, pegboard and plywood for sure," I say, and pretend not to notice Ashley whip around when she hears my voice.

"Or maybe that's part of our next mission,"

Jasper says. McKenna's face crinkles up in confusion. "Mabel and her grampa go on these scavenging hunts, and she took me on one. It was awesome, but we could look for some of this stuff too?"

"That'd be great. Think you could find a toaster?" McKenna asks while I nod.

"He already has at least two toasters," I say.

"What if that's our end goal? Pushing down the toaster's lever. We might need to have something pretty heavy fall to have enough force to turn it on," McKenna says.

"He also has at least two bowling balls," I say.

McKenna and Jasper laugh. We spend the rest of the period planning, and I don't look over when Farrah and Ashley leave the room.

The whole afternoon, I think about how differently Jasper and McKenna reacted to my and Grampa's hunts. On the bus I don't sit across from Ashley and Farrah. I decide to go to the back, and Jasper and McKenna sit by me. But every time I think about what Farrah said and how Ashley laughed, it hurts.

When I get home, I sit and stare at my phone.

Today, I have to bike to Grampa's, pick up the wagon, and then ride over to Archie's.

Until recently, Grampa and I always visited Archie at least once a week, and it feels like I have to go today, like if I don't go, I'm giving up one more piece of Grampa. Plus, I have a business proposition to make. But I don't want to go alone.

I pick up my phone, call to make sure Archie's open, and then text Jasper.

13

I WAIT FIVE MINUTES, UNSURE IF HE'LL SHOW up, before I see Jasper pedaling toward me.

He comes to a stop and unbuckles his bike helmet. "Hey, sorry I'm late. I've never been here before."

"It's one of my favorite places," I say.

He looks around the parking lot and raises an unimpressed eyebrow. "You brought the stuff we found?"

"I thought Archie—he owns the store—might resell it for us."

Jasper shakes his head. "Not us. You. I'm just here for the adventure."

"Why *are* you helping me anyway?" I ask.

"What else do I have to do?" He shrugs, hops off his bike, and heads toward the store. "You coming?" he asks. I hustle to catch up, sure he's not telling me the whole truth about why he's so ready to tag along.

The happy chimes on the door have hardly had a chance to quit ringing before Archie comes and wraps me in a hug. He likes to wear fancy clothes, so his hugs feel sort of like being rolled up in a wool blanket—comfy at first, then a little scratchy.

"Sorry I haven't made it by lately," I say.

"You know what, your Mom actually came in. I haven't seen her in years." Archie holds me by the shoulders and scans me from head to toe. "How are you doing?"

"Okay, I guess."

Archie nods like he understands all I'm not saying. "I stopped by when he was in the hospital, and I'm planning on paying him a visit tomorrow at Whispering Pines. Just haven't had a chance to make it over." He turns toward Jasper. "And who's this?"

"This is Jasper," I say. "He's primarily interested in books." I realize that I'm not sure what else Jasper is interested in. "And science," I add, but it sounds like a question.

Archie claps. "Oh, I have a treat for you. Follow me." He scans Jasper's outfit and says, "I have a hat collection in aisle four that might interest you." Archie is older than Grampa, but he moves fast. He takes off before Jasper can answer.

I smile. At least something has stayed the same. "I'll meet you there in a sec," I say. Jasper nods and runs after Archie.

The glassware aisle still has many of the same things it did the last time I was here with Grampa. Still, I start my slow walk, opening my heart up. But it's not working. Suddenly, I feel like coming was a bad idea. It's not until I look down, trying to think up some excuse to leave, that I see patches of blue flash and fade on the floor. There on the very end of the shelf sit four heavy glass dessert bowls, the antique kind with a dish sitting on top of a pedestal, and so deep blue they immediately remind me of Mom's A Night in Paradise table.

I pick one up and wait to see if I feel anything special. As I turn the glass, I think about Mom and how little she and I have in common. Maybe that could change. Maybe these bowls could be the first step. Maybe a change here and there wouldn't be the worst thing.

They're not exactly heart-find material, but they do spark some possibilities.

A few flea bites are scattered along the base of one, but the other three are perfect. A flea bite is glassware lingo for teeny, tiny chips—no actual bugs involved. Besides, Mom only has to do two place settings for the competition. If Lorna Diamond can win with vintage glass on her table, then why can't Mom?

Jasper rounds a corner with an armload of books and a bowler hat balanced on top of his stack. "Whoa. Those are cool." He nods toward the bowls.

I hold one in the light again and remind myself to remember he likes books, science, *and* hats. "Maybe they belonged to a duchess."

Jasper's eyes go wide. "An exiled duchess."

I nod. "Or maybe they belonged to quadruplet sisters. One for each."

Jasper's big smile comes out. "Locked in a tower by an evil, exiled duchess."

I hold one of the bowls close to his face. "And

they eventually poison the duchess using this very vessel."

Jasper shudders as he stares at the bowl. "Too real."

We look up at each other and crack up laughing.

There's one problem. The whole set is thirty-five dollars, which is a little high, but I don't haggle over prices with Archie. Plus, I only have a twenty and I need to keep every last cent for Grampa.

"You go on and take those." Archie makes his way toward us with a feather duster. "Your grampa always donates so much, I owe him." He picks up the other two bowls and says, "Come on up to the register when you're ready."

"Archie really wanted me to pick a hat. What do you think?" I turn back to Jasper, and the hat's pushed his curls over his face so that just his nose and big smile are showing.

He may be joking but I ask what Grampa would if he were here. "When you have it on do you feel different in a good way? Like wearing it makes you feel bigger inside?"

Jasper brushes his curls back. "You know, I think so."

"Then you should get it." I head to the register and Jasper follows.

As Archie wraps the dessert bowls, he says, "The previous owner told me that the cut in the glass is called Moon and Stars. And he gave me another story for my book." Archie nods to the beat-up notebook he keeps by the register. "You find anything to add to yours lately?"

"What book?" Jasper asks. I almost shake my head at Archie. But instead, I bite my lip and hope for the best.

"Sometimes people have a hard time parting with something, and they have a special story they want to tell. An item can be a connection to someone or to an important moment." Archie holds up the tattered composition notebook. "I write all their stories in here. A lot of times, I fill in the details. What Mabel's Grampa would call my 'right to historical whimsy.'" He tucks his notebook back behind the register.

I sigh with relief, but then he goes on. "Mabel keeps one too. She's a true collector. I even told her my own story and am happy to have the honor of being her very first entry. She came up with the term *heart find* and I think it's a perfect fit." My cheeks are practically on fire. Archie looks over at me and winks.

I hold out my money, eager to change the topic. "Let me at least pay half."

"Nope. I won't take a penny. Maybe those dishes will end up being special for you." He holds my hand for a second before giving it a squeeze and letting go.

Jasper pays for his books and his new hat, then clears his throat and nods toward my bike parked outside.

"Archie," I say. "I have a favor to ask. I have some stuff that I was wondering if I could sell here. You can take a percentage of the profits."

"That's not normally how I do things." Archie cranes his neck and looks out at my wagon. "Tell me what you've got."

When I finish listing all we found, Archie says, "Brand-new baby merchandise would definitely sell." He nods. "Go on and bring it in."

Jasper and I carry in the milk crates, and Archie

shows us where to unload them. Once we're done, our items take up four shelves in the kids' section.

"I'll put the money aside for you," Archie says. "And I won't be taking any percentage."

"Thanks, I owe you one." This time I give him a hug before he beats me to it.

As we walk toward our bikes, Jasper says, "I like Archie. I think it's cool that he keeps that notebook." Jaspers motions to the front window. "That display shows he's someone who likes a good story."

"We work on the windows together. Grampa and I normally come here a few times a week." It's been a struggle to get back to thinking positive, but I'm close. "Hey, since I didn't spend my money, want to go over to Joe's and get some fries and a soda? My treat." I point to Joe's Diner a few doors down. After all Jasper's done, I can spare a few dollars to say thank you.

Once we're in a booth, Jasper sorts through his stack of paperbacks. "Look at this cover." He holds up one called *The Snow Queen* by Joan D. Vinge that shows a woman in a headdress of white feathers and pearls. "I couldn't resist it. She's giving off serious White Witch vibes."

"You would've liked my mom's Frozen Wonderland table. She made a centerpiece that looks a lot like that fancy bonnet but crammed in a vase."

Jasper laughs. "So, my mom has your mom's business card. How exactly does someone become a 'table setting artist'?"

I shrug. "A lifelong love of perfection and competition? Everything has to be just so. If a soup spoon is a fraction of an inch out of place, it's counted off the score."

"Really?" He takes a fry and blows on it before dipping it in so much ketchup it droops.

I nod. "She's judged on creativity, originality, use of color, interpretation of theme, correctness, and presentation. One year, my mom lost first place because her butter-spreading knife wasn't exactly at a forty-five-degree angle across the bread plate." I switch to a whisper. "She even has a nemesis."

Jasper leans over. "Like an archenemy?"

"Yep. This one lady beats her every time. Not by much. But that doesn't seem to matter." I take a slurp of my soda. "Mom has regionals near the end of October, and if she places there, she'll be able to do the National Expo the week after that. It's what she calls 'The Big Show.' Years of trying and she's never made it in before." I grab the ketchup. "Hey, why are you really helping me? Also, the bowler hat looks good. Did you know the bowler hat was more popular in the West than the cowboy hat or the sombrero? Everybody wore them, from Charlie Chaplin to Billy the Kid. One of Charlie Chaplin's sold at auction for almost seventy thousand dollars."

"That's why I'm helping you. That right there." Jasper laughs, leans forward, looks me straight in the eye, and adjusts his glasses. "I moved from Chicago a few months ago. And I hated it here. No Lake Michigan, no Harold Washington Library, no deep dish." He looks out the window a minute and I wonder if he's thinking *no friends* or if that's just me. He motions to the short one-story buildings and parking lots. "Everything's just so…ordinary. But, I don't know, you make ordinary seem unusual. Sounds like your mom does too."

I snort. "My mom and I aren't all that much alike."

Jasper shrugs. "Anyways, you're not the first person to call me different. I've always been able to get along better with grown-ups like my mom's patients. I like a person who isn't afraid to be themself."

My cheeks warm. I didn't realize how badly I needed to hear someone say they liked me. "Do you want to go? To the competition, I mean." I ask before I think it through. "I'll have to check with my mom, but she probably won't care."

"Why not?" Jasper says, and shows me that big smile of his again.

On the way home, I bike past four dumpsters all lined up in the strip mall's parking lot and think of the four dessert bowls tucked away in my bag and the four shelves full of my baby stuff. Today, it finally feels like something amazing could be waiting just around the corner. All I have to do is keep looking.

14

LIKE EVERYTHING LATELY, THE CAFETERIA IS THE
same but not. Ashley's already sitting with Farrah by
the time I line up. They hunch behind their lunch
boxes whispering and shooting looks over to where
David Verdon sits with a loud group of his friends. Last
night, Mom and I had dinner with Grampa. Mom got
takeout from the Icon. It wasn't quite the same, but it
wasn't too bad. Mr. Curtis joined us, Grampa laughed
out loud three times, and Mom even joined in once.
I'd rather be back in the Whispering Pines cafeteria
than here.

Mrs. Kirkpatrick keeps us busy enough that Ashley ignoring me first period is bearable. But by lunchtime, there's no pretending everything is fine.

I smile back at Mrs. Brandon as she doles out my chicken nuggets. When I turn toward table 4, Jasper and McKenna are deep into chatting, maybe about something Rube Goldberg related. Sitting in a certain row on the bus is one thing but changing tables in the cafeteria is like a public declaration that my friendship with Ashley is over.

I stand there for a minute with my tray, looking from one table to the other, and think about the first time Grampa broke our number one rule: Don't climb into dumpsters. Aside from being disgusting, there's a chance of injury. Plus, there are some new dumpsters that have a locking motorized lid and a compressor; it'd be like getting stuck in a smaller version of the trash compactor in *Return of the Jedi*. But once Grampa and I opened up what turned out to be a mostly empty dumpster. Empty, except for the bottom, which was littered with marbles. Grampa tucked his lips into a thin line and said,

"Sometimes the risk is worth the reward." Then he climbed in.

Friends seem every bit as hard to pass up as marbles. I tuck my lips into a thin line, walk over, and sit down by Jasper.

"So, Mom said we can pick you up before her competition. It's still almost three weeks away, but she likes to plan in advance. She'll check in with your mom about it when she goes to visit Grampa today."

Jasper claps. "I already asked. My mom and dad are so happy I'm making friends here, I think they'd let me go anywhere. What's the theme again?"

"A Night in Paradise." I pop a whole nugget in my mouth.

"Oh, sounds like the prom. If you could make a table, what would it be?" McKenna asks. "Mine would have something to do with rainbows. And I don't mean like rainbows and unicorns, but refraction, reflection, and dispersion of light. Imagine it." McKenna waggles her fingers in the air. "Eating in a natural phenomenon."

Jasper stares at me for a second of quiet before

we all crack up. But it's not in a mean way. McKenna laughs too.

"What about you? Has your mom ever let you pick her theme?" McKenna asks.

I almost choke on a nugget and manage to shake my head. "There are only a few competitions where the tablescaper gets to choose the theme. But Mom plans her tables for months. She'd never let me pick." I chew and think. "But I'd set the whole table with items that were special, somehow tell a story, not just stuff I ordered online." If it were only me and Jasper, I might bring up heart finds.

But it's like Jasper thinks of it too. "Oh, hey, what'd your mom say about the bowls? Did she love them?" he asks.

I shrug. "I haven't shown her yet. She probably won't use them."

Jasper scrunches his face. "Why not? They're beautiful. Besides, her table theme is A Night in Paradise and the bowls were called Moon and Stars. Seems like a perfect fit."

"Maybe," I say, but Mom's version of perfect means flawless and definitely not preowned.

"Hmm. It wouldn't be too hard to do with a properly placed light source. What are the rules on that?" McKenna rubs her chin, lost in thought.

"There can't be anything on the floor," I say.

Jasper laughs. "She's stuck on her rainbow table."

I nod as McKenna furrows her brow.

"What about hanging from the ceiling?" she asks.

"I'm pretty sure that's against the rules too."

"Hmm," she says. "If the whole table were done in white and the centerpiece was made entirely of prisms *and* we put a light source in the middle, it could still work."

McKenna talks the whole rest of lunch about science-themed tables. She is going on about one where everything emits steam, achieved by heating a wet tablecloth. I suggest all the items on the menu are served steamed as well.

"It could look like a rain forest," I say.

"Perfect." McKenna's eyes go wide. "I can see it. Can't you? Ferns and orchids and vines everywhere. Think your mom would go for it?"

No way, no how. "Maybe."

"Oh, we could get some dry ice and create a little

fog. Forget Rube Goldberg machines, let's change the face of tablescaping." McKenna bangs the table and Jasper and I laugh. I leave lunch feeling better than I have all week.

We pick up our conversation as soon as I get on the bus, and when we approach Whispering Pines Jasper stands and says, "This is me."

"Hey, maybe I could get off here Monday and visit Grampa," I say.

"You totally should. On bingo day the prizes are Jell-O, pudding, and lottery scratch-off tickets. Most exciting spot in town." We wave to each other once he's on the sidewalk. It's the first time that seeing Whispering Pines doesn't feel strange. Maybe it's thinking of Jasper there with Grampa.

At my stop, Ashley gets off and walks toward her house without looking back, but the only reason I notice is because I turn around to wave to McKenna.

I walk in, toss my backpack onto the couch, and notice another one of Mom's books on the counter. *Move Forward with Forward Thinking* and only two sticky notes this time. I roll my eyes just as Mom bursts through the front door.

"Help," she mumbles behind a tower of boxes.

Our dining table is set up in a trial run for her A Night in Paradise competition. In no time Mom has unboxed her new purchases and stands with one hand on her hip and her mouth in a concentrated pucker. She crouches at the corner of the table, closes one eye, then walks around and repeats her inspection at another corner before asking, "Hey, hon. How was your day?"

"It was actually great."

Mom pauses to look up at me. "That's good news." She points to the table. "What do you think? I was up all night trying to get the crystal placement to look random but also purposeful."

How can something be random and on purpose at the same time? I reach to touch one of the larger crystals, and Mom swats my hand. "Not until I take a photo. I've got about three weeks left to really make this table shine, but I just don't think I've found the spark yet, know what I mean? There's a lot riding on this win."

"Hmm," I say, because I don't have a clue.

"What do you think of the new addition?" She

motions to a fresh-from-the-box silver telescope rising from the middle of her centerpiece. It reminds me of a submarine's periscope emerging from the sea. The telescope isn't real. Judging from the box, she found it on DiscountDeskDécor.com. What good is a telescope that will never see a single star?

"Jasper is really excited about regionals," I say.

"I'm glad you're making some new friends." Mom smiles as she gets out her phone to document the placement of everything. "Look at this." She shows me a picture. "I've been working on it for weeks at Pattie's. It may be my best showstopper yet." It's a giant globe in solid navy and covered in delicate silver drawings of constellations. She does some of her trial runs in the back room at Pattie's. Sometimes I don't see all that Mom's cooked up for a table until we set it.

"I have something to show you too. Just a sec." I rush to my room. They're still covered in newspaper, on the floor at the foot of my bed. I carry the dessert bowls into the kitchen, place them on the counter, and slowly unwrap each one, waiting for Mom to notice. She makes her way to the last corner of the table and squints, moving her head from side to side like one of those dancing cobras in a basket.

Mom only looks up after I make a big show of clearing my throat. I've done a little research on the bowls since I got them. "These are from the L. E. Smith Glass Company. The cut in the glass is called 'Moon and Stars,' and these are special because they're marked." I lift one up and turn it over for Mom to see the little *S*, *G*, and *C* insignia on the bottom. "Not exactly a one-of-a-kind, but still unique."

"They're pretty," Mom says. "I bet Grampa would love to hear all about them tonight at dinner." Mom adjusts a single crystal, steps back to eye it, and then takes more pictures. "I can't believe I'm one win away from my first appearance at the Expo. I've been dreaming up a table for the National Expo for three years. My mock-up is at the store, but Pattie thinks something is missing. Wait until you see it. I've made the centerpiece out of real leather cowboy boots!"

"They're in near perfect condition." I motion to the dessert bowls again and try to open my heart up and hope that maybe something special will happen. But Mom is too focused on adjusting her silverware. "Only one has the tiniest of nicks around the base. Good thing you only have to do two table settings."

Mom's checking the placement of her soup spoon with a ruler. She's humming Taylor Swift's "Shake It Off"; that song is like her anthem.

"I think they're perfect for your table."

That gets Mom's attention. She straightens, her face stuck somewhere between shock and fear. "This table?"

"You said you wanted to do some of these competitions *together*." I grab the back of one of the barstools. "Well, this is my idea to make your table stand out from the rest. To make it more than perfect."

Mom crosses her arms and blows an escaped curl out of her face. "Mabel, there's nothing wrong with perfect. For goodness' sake, that's what the word means." She grabs her measuring tape. "Besides that, I wouldn't want to break up your set."

She clicks the button, begins measuring the

drape of the tablecloth, and doesn't even seem to notice when I leave.

I plop onto my bed. Moments later Mom knocks, but this time she doesn't come in. "I'm sorry, honey. I didn't mean to hurt your feelings." Her voice is muffled by the door. "But I could start my own business with a national win under my belt, not to mention what opportunities might come from an appearance on *Top Table*. I'm not sure it's the right time to take chances. Want to talk about it?"

"No," I say, and hear her sigh before she walks away.

My Amberina basket flickers its colors on my bedspread before they dwindle away in the late afternoon sun. All the good feelings from my day, from Jasper and McKenna, fade too.

I need Grampa back home, and baby clothes aren't going to do the trick.

Holiday season is closing in and that means shelves will be restocked with Halloween, Thanksgiving, and even Christmas merchandise, getting rid of the old to make room for the new. There's only one spot in Abner close enough for me to bike where there are stores all crammed together.

One haul from the dumpsters at the Merkle Creek Mall and I'll show Mom I can make a difference. Like Grampa said, sometimes the risk is worth the reward. Trash to cash, here I come.

15

MONDAY AFTERNOON, JASPER AND I GET OFF THE
bus and walk to Whispering Pines together. Another
whole weekend with no hunts, no finds, no trash-to-
treasure projects, and I've been in a mood all day.
Jasper bumps me with his elbow and says, "You don't
have to tell me what's wrong if you don't want to. But
I just thought I'd let you know you could. If you feel
like it."

I kick at fallen leaves and keep my eyes on the
ground. "I just want Grampa back home, and sometimes I worry that whatever I do, I won't get back to

the way things were. Grampa always says if it can be broken, it can be fixed. But I don't know anymore."

Jasper stops walking for a minute.

"What?" I ask.

"Never mind," he says, and gives me a smile that's small and tight.

It's my turn to stop walking. "What is it?"

"You know I live with my grandma?"

I shake my head.

"My dad got injured and then fired. So, we moved here to live with my grandma because she knows the director of the nursing home and got Mom this job. Now we all live in the house my mom grew up in. It's okay, but it'll never be like it was before; it can't be *fixed*." Jasper shrugs. "I have to accept it. My mom says we have to think of ways to make right now better instead of wishing we could go backward."

"I'm sorry, Jasper," I say.

Jasper nods. "But this, making money to help you, is different. This we can do something about." He smiles. "And like you said, you never know what we might find."

I nod and smile back and stare up ahead at

Whispering Pines. What if he's right though, and this whole mess is something that can't be fixed no matter how hard I try?

"So, what's our next mission?" he asks.

"The mall on Sunday afternoon. We'll have to be extra careful."

Jasper nods. "Why extra careful?"

"Well, there are security guards there. They work inside the mall, but if they see us, they might ask us to leave." Maybe it's because I'm afraid he won't go with me, but I don't tell Jasper that Grampa and I've never been there together. Whatever Grampa's reasons for staying away, they can't be more important than my reason for going.

There's a man in mint green scrubs working the front desk this time. He's on the phone when he buzzes us in to Whispering Pines, and as we pass by, he holds out a hand for Jasper to high-five.

The custodian walks past the elevators as we get on.

"Hi, Mr. Jeffries," Jasper says.

"Hey there, Jasper." He points a finger in our direction. "Don't cause any trouble today."

"Can't make any promises," Jasper says. As the doors close, Mr. Jeffries cracks up.

We get off on the third floor and are met by a woman waiting to go down. "Well, if it isn't my favorite young man," she says.

"Good afternoon, Ms. Flannigan. You're looking lovely as always," Jasper says.

"And you're an excellent fibber." She taps Jasper gently with her cane. "And that's why you're my favorite young man."

We walk toward the social room. I can't quit staring at him. "You're like a celebrity here."

He switches to a whisper. "I'm very popular with the older generation. It's my favorite part of Mom's job. A person who's lived a long life is full of stories, and I love a good story. Besides, some of the residents are a little lonely. It feels good to keep them company."

One of the staff members is setting up for bingo, and the social room is packed. Grampa sits at a table with Mr. Curtis and four ladies. The look on his face when he sees me loosens what's left of the tightness I've been carrying around.

"Mae-mae, I didn't know you were coming," Grampa says. His smile droops on the right side, but it's big and the best thing I've seen all day. "And good to see you again, Jasper." Grampa's words are slower than usual, but it's better than it was just a few days ago.

Jasper reaches across the table and shakes Grampa's hand, then turns to me. "I'm going to say hi to Mom and I'll meet you back here." He looks at Grampa and says, "I can't wait to hear about another one of your finds."

"Can't wait to tell you about one," Grampa says. This takes me by surprise, that Grampa and Jasper have been swapping stories. Does that mean Grampa's been lonely? Jasper waves and jogs down the hall, his sneakers squeaking.

I didn't tell Jasper not to let Grampa know about our visit to the Baby of Mine dumpster. Grampa thinks trash-to-cash hauls are less about inspiration and more about digging through garbage looking for something that might be worth money. He's right, but how's inspiration supposed to save his house and get him out of this place?

I walk around the table toward the empty seat next to Grampa, the guilt of keeping secrets from him slowing me down, when Grampa stands! No wheelchair. He's using a cane with four prongs on the bottom. I pounce across the short distance between us and give him a gentle hug.

"You can squeeze harder. I won't break." Grampa laughs. And suddenly I start crying right there in front of all the residents gathering for bingo. It's just a few tears, but I bury my head into Grampa's sweater. He pats my back. "There now. Come on."

He leads me down the hall to his room and settles on the edge of his bed. I sit in a chair facing him.

"Want to tell me what's been going on?"

When Grampa and I were on our searches, I would sometimes talk the whole time and he'd just listen. I don't know if it's because I've wanted to tell Mom about Ashley and haven't or if it's just that I haven't been alone with Grampa in so long, but everything loosens and spills out. I tell Grampa about Farrah and the matching shirts and the miserable bus rides. And how being with Mom feels so lonely because we don't understand each other.

Even though I'm telling Grampa all these horrible things, it feels so close to normal that I hardly feel sad. In fact, it's nice to say them all out loud.

"It's like Ashley went to camp and now she's different." It's also that Grampa isn't around, and all the things I like to do, things we used to do together, are different now too, and I'm scared they won't ever be the way they were again. But I don't say any of that because I don't want to make Grampa feel worse than he already must.

Grampa frowns. "I've known Ashley since she was little, and she doesn't seem different. *She* seems the same." My confusion must show because he goes on. "Some people spend a lot of time trying to fit in. And some people follow their hearts instead of everyone else." Grampa sighs. "I know it's hard, but things change. And it's okay to move on but appreciate the good times you two had." It takes Grampa a long time to get all that out. Talking is hard work for him; some words come easy, but some are a struggle.

I sigh. "It feels so weird to have her not like me anymore."

Grampa harrumphs and crosses his arms. "If

being well liked means being like everyone else, I'd rather be unpopular."

"Well, you're not in sixth grade."

"True enough." He smiles at me. "You remind me so much of your gramma. She was an original too—quick-witted, strong-willed, clever but believed in impossible things." He looks over at Dr. Jon perched on the windowsill and casting a larger-than-life shadow on the floor. "You know she thought that old thing was magical, like Aladdin's lamp? She said she used up all three wishes in one day, which was just the sort of thing she'd do." I've heard this story before, but I go ahead and listen again.

"As for you and your mom, well, I'm the last person to ask about that." Grampa looks out the small window of his room.

"Why didn't you ever go to her competitions?" I ask.

"The pageants were always her and her mom's thing." He shrugs. "It just wasn't for me. I wanted her to know she doesn't have to win something to be special."

I think about how Mom hates the collecting I do

with Grampa, but she never says so. She always listens about my finds and even pretends to like them sometimes.

"You should probably tell her that," I say.

"You're right." Grampa nods just as there's a quiet knock at the door.

"Hey." Jasper leans his head in. "They're about to start. You still want to play?"

Grampa uses his cane to rise, and once he's up, we walk down the hall together. Jasper tells us about the last time he won, and Mrs. Wingfield protested because he wasn't an actual resident.

"The prize was a vanilla pudding cup. But she was ready to throw down. No joke."

Grampa and I laugh so loud and hard that we turn heads, and Jasper's big smile is full blast.

By the time we make it back to the social room there're just a few seats left. A woman narrows her eyes as we walk by. Jasper whispers, "That's Mrs. Wingfield." I giggle all the way to the table.

"You coming to the Halloween party?" Grampa asks. The social director makes her way around to all the tables, passing out cards. When she gets to us, she scans the room and whispers to Jasper, "Mrs. Wingfield has OT in five minutes, so I think it's safe today."

"Told you." Jasper takes his card.

"There's a party?" I ask.

Grampa nods while Jasper answers. "My mom says it's a big deal. Every year Mrs. Hayden, the social director, comes up with a theme and the residents do a performance. The local news covers it. This year they're dancing to 'Thriller' by Michael Jackson. She said she and your mom are teaming up to volunteer."

"Wait, that old video with the zombies?" The bingo game starts, so we continue our conversation in whispers.

Grampa and Jasper nod. "I've got a starring role," Grampa says, and holds his arms out and groans like the walking dead. "We have rehearsals and everything."

Jasper bumps me with his shoulder. "Come on. It'll be fun. It's the same night as the school's Fall Festival. We could go to both."

"The Fall Festival is a costume party," I say. I think of Ashley and Farrah's half-hearted invitation for me to dress up as a character I've never heard of. The way they included me makes me feel even more left out.

"Well, then we better come up with some costumes soon." Jasper purses his lips. "Who's your favorite character from a book?"

"Captain Underpants," Grampa says. Someone at the front of the room yells "Bingo!"

"Grampa!" I almost kick him under the table. "That was from second grade."

Jasper is busy laughing.

"Before she did anything she'd yell 'Tra-la-la!'" Grampa is laughing now too.

I go ahead and gently nudge him with my foot.

"I know exactly who I'm going as," Jasper says. He holds a hand up. "Don't tell me yours. Let's meet there and surprise each other."

"Deal," I say. But now that I think about it, Ashley normally decides what our costumes will be. In fact, she made most of the decisions. Well, I can make decisions too.

Jasper nudges me. "What did you say the other day? The best things are unexpected."

Grampa nods and points a finger at Jasper. "Bingo," he says.

Jasper and I both roll our eyes and then laugh.

Grampa smiles, but he also sends me a strange look. Then I realize Jasper's quote might've revealed too much. Grampa only said that when we'd go on extreme treasure hunts.

Jasper's mom rounds the corner with her bag and coat and approaches our table. She points to Jasper. "Sorry, bud, we have to cut bingo short today. Your dad needs the van. Nice to see you again, Mabel." She turns to Grampa. "And I'll see you bright and early for our session tomorrow."

Grampa gives her a salute as Jasper rises and says, "See you in the morning."

As they leave, Grampa narrows his eyes at me and says, "Just don't do anything I wouldn't do."

At least he's not going to tell Mom. And then like magic, the elevator bell dings and out steps Mom carrying a small tower of takeout containers.

Grampa gives my hand a squeeze. "Seems like you've found a friend who likes you just the way you are."

Mom walks over. "What'd I miss?"

"I was saying it's hard to fit in when you're one of a kind," Grampa says.

"Are we talking about you or Mabel, because in my book you're both definitely originals." It's unclear if Mom means this as a compliment.

Grampa laughs out loud, and I feel like I might cry again. Not because I'm sad, but because for the first time since Grampa's stroke, I feel like our old normal might not be so far away after all.

16

THE OKLAHOMA CITY CONVENTION CENTER IS A huge metal building with concrete floors. The walkways are lined with booths, because there's also a handmade jewelry and homemade jam convention. Grampa would definitely say it was jam-packed.

I've been to this festival ever since Mom started to compete. A memory of Ashley with us a few years ago pushes into my head. We sampled so much jam that Mom joked our fingers would be permanently stuck together. This year is sure turning out to be different. I look over at Jasper, and he smiles. Maybe sometimes new isn't all that bad.

It's warm for late October, and the air-conditioning units roar like beehives. Jasper leans over and whispers, "What about She-Ra?"

I shake my head and laugh. "My ideas are kind of out there, but no one will be wearing the same costume as me. Besides, I thought you didn't want to know?" Despite Jasper telling me to keep my costume a surprise, he spent a few weeks trying to guess and now has moved on to suggestions.

"Or Katniss." Jasper's eyes are wide. "Will they let you bring a Nerf bow into the gym? Probably not."

Now that I'm not limited to best friend costumes, I actually have a lot of ideas. Not a one is a character from a book and there's no way I'm telling.

Mom's heels echo with each step, and Jasper's grin grows wider the closer we get to the roped-off area containing twenty tables. Mom's is table 17.

I shudder from a chill just as Lorna Diamond's sequined blazer catches my eye. She parks herself at table 16. Never in all our competitions has Lorna been our neighbor.

"I can't wait to see your centerpiece!" Jasper

practically dances in place. I cut my eyes at him. "What? This is the most exciting thing I've been a part of since the incident with Mrs. Wingfield at bingo."

"Well, you won't have to wait much longer." Mom's smile is tight as she slides a box our way. "But linens first."

Mom and I picked up Jasper first thing this morning. They immediately hit it off. Jasper asked Mom where she got her inspiration, and they talked the whole short drive. Jasper seems to fit right in with my family.

He looks over at Lorna and then at me. I give him a single nod. I've told him all about her and her glitzy jackets. I take the steamer while Jasper holds up Mom's tablecloth by the corners. He whispers, "The suspense... I couldn't have written it any better."

After we've steamed the creases out, Mom hands me a bottle of glass cleaner. "A little help?" I can tell from the tightness in her voice that Jasper and I aren't the only ones to notice our sparkly neighbor.

Mom's hand shakes as she reaches to open one of her suitcases. Seems like she wasn't so prepared for Lorna to be within spitting distance. I wonder if she's feeling like I did on the bus and needs a reminder that she isn't alone.

I go over and put my hand on hers for a second. "It'll be perfect, just like you want."

Mom smiles at me and takes the cloth from Jasper; it's a velvety blue that's somewhere between navy and cobalt. I help with the silverware, polishing each piece to an extra-high shine.

Mom keeps side-eyeing me. "What did I do now?" I ask.

She starts slowly unrolling something from Bubble Wrap. I almost fall over when I see the first flash of cobalt blue glass.

"I knew you'd use them. Don't they look like they came straight from Narnia?" Jasper says to Mom and goes back to unwrapping the bread plates as though Mom didn't just this very minute do the most un-Mom-like thing in the entire world.

One other person seems every bit as shocked as

me—Lorna Diamond. She does a double take with such force she's lucky she doesn't get whiplash. The look on her face is one I've never seen there before. Worry.

Once we've unpacked everything and Mom goes around with her measuring tape, Jasper and I take a step back and scan our work. The antique dessert bowls are exactly the same shade as the velvet table-cloth, so much so that it takes a squint or two to see where one ends and the other begins. All the objects vary in height and remind me of city skyscrapers. The touches of silver shine here and there in a place-ment that looks both accidental and flawless, like a starry night.

Mom joins us and we stand together, admiring the table.

"We've got an hour until the judging. Want to find some food that is both delicious and terrible for us?" she asks. Jasper and I laugh and nod.

Mom and I never stay for the judging. It's too nerve-racking to watch them walk around and whis-per. Another thing we never do is go get junk food, but Mom's mood is better than I've ever seen it.

She's humming "Shake It Off" all the way to the food court. Jasper joins in and then I do too. We only stop to giggle, Mom included.

We head straight for the stand that reeks the strongest of fried food and sugar. There's a line, and ahead of us are two girls wearing shirts like Ashley and Farrah's with ROCKSTARZ printed across the back. One of them turns around and points to a booth. It's not some girl in a similar shirt. It's Ashley.

"Look who's here!" Mom says, all excited and happy. She waves to them before I can stop her. Farrah fake smiles and waves back, but Ashley looks like she'd rather disappear. After they get their order, they walk over. Ashley always orders fried Oreos, so I know what's on her plate without looking.

Mom gives Ashley an awkward hug. "Hey, sweetheart, what have you been up to? I haven't seen you in ages."

Ashley's neck is slowly going from pink to patchy red. "Yeah. I've been spending more time at my dad's. He had a meeting near here today. So, we talked him into bringing us."

"Oh," Mom says.

"Hey, Mabel," Ashley says. "Hey, Jasper."

"Hey," Jasper answers, while I only manage a small smile.

"Good luck today." Ashley starts to back away. I spot her dad on his phone sitting at a table in the food court.

Farrah pulls on Ashley's arm. "Well, see ya," she says, and walks off toward a stand selling beaded jewelry.

Mom's face is full of questions, but rather than ask them she puts a hand on my shoulder and looks me straight in my eyes. "Let's get good and sugared up." She smiles and gives me a little squeeze.

When we head back an hour later, Jasper's teeth are pale blue from the cotton candy. Each score is posted on a folded card next to the menu. Scores are broken down into categories. Twenty-five points for Tangible Standards—this includes stuff like the condition, stability, and quality of the materials used. Twenty-five points for Aesthetic Standards, meaning creativity, originality, and interpretation of the theme. The majority of the score, fifty points, comes from the Elements and Principles section.

Elements and Principles is make-or-break territory when it comes to winning and completely up to the judges. Tables are marked for line, use of space, color, texture, and unity. This system is a mystery. If one judge thinks the centerpiece is too high and another thinks it's too low, well, they can both take off a point. And when you're up against Lorna Diamond, every point counts.

I hold my breath as we approach Mom's table. Jasper stands so close that his upper arm rests against mine. Mom blocks my view of the score card, but she whispers, "I can't believe this." And then her shoulders start to shake a little. Maybe the dessert bowls weren't a good idea after all.

When mom turns around, she is wiping tears from the corners of her eyes before they have a chance to smear her mascara, and finally I see her card. One hundred points. A perfect score.

Lorna is doling out high-fives and handshakes like she's already won. The look on her face when she finally sees Mom's score makes me laugh out loud. But then I see she also got perfect marks. It's a tie.

A woman in a peach pantsuit approaches Mom and Lorna. She sticks out a thin hand in Lorna's direction and then after a quick shake extends it to Mom, saying, "Denise Harding, head judge this year, and it seems I have the job of delivering both some good and bad news. The good news is that you've accomplished something never done in the thirty-year history of this competition, a tie for Best of Show. The bad news is we've only got one ribbon. I've spoken with the sponsor and they're willing to up the prize money so the two of you can split it. We'll order another ribbon, but it won't arrive for a week or so. That means you'll have to agree on who gets the one we do have. Or you both can wait, and we'll mail them out."

Lorna takes a step forward. "Denise, let's go ahead and give the ribbon to Jane. Lord knows, I can wait a few weeks to add another to my collection." Mom's smile twitches the tiniest bit, and just like that Lorna takes Mom's win and makes it mean a little less.

I'm tired of feeling less than, and I don't want Mom feeling that way for a single minute after winning for the first time. I turn to Lorna. "This is only Mom's fourth year to compete." I smile as innocently as possible. "Were you in that first competition sixty years ago?"

Lorna's plastered-on grin fades faster than a smear of Windex on glass. Jasper snorts and Denise chuckles quietly and says, "Thirty years ago, dear. No, Lorna wasn't but I was. Lorna came along after and has been winning ever since. Almost fifteen years, I believe?"

Lorna only manages a curt nod.

"Whoa, I wasn't even born yet," I say. Mom gives me a gentle elbow to let me know I've gone far enough. Jasper's big grin is shining bright.

For the rest of the day, Mom's humming of "Shake It Off" is the soundtrack to everything else, and Jasper and I chat and laugh the whole ride home like we've been friends for years instead of weeks. I

look over at Jasper, who is now shimmying and singing "Shake It Off" out loud to accompany Mom's
humming. He bumps me with his shoulder. I groan
but join in. Seeing Ashley was a tiny flea bite in my
day, but there were also a few pretty good finds.

17

MOM HAS AN EARLY-AFTERNOON WEDDING. SHE'S already dressed and almost out the door when I come into the kitchen. She gives me a quick hug and says, "Sorry, hon, I've got to run and we're about out of groceries. There's some rice cakes and an orange. Love you, and Mrs. Hammons is on call. If you need anything at all just give her a ring. I'll be back before dinner." She blows me a kiss and rushes off to work.

As soon as she's gone, I run to my room and take the spider pin from my backpack and give it a little kiss before attaching it inside my shirt pocket again. On my way out, I text Grampa's address to Jasper and ask him to meet me there instead of at the mall. We need the extra wagon just in case. After Mom's surprise perfect score yesterday, I'm feeling like I might get lucky.

When I arrive, Jasper is already there, inspecting Grampa's mailbox, the post made from an old water pump. I pull to a stop and Jasper motions to the garage wall, where Grampa's hung three old windows complete with flower-filled planters. Jasper turns in a slow circle. "This place is amazing."

I nod. "That's nothing. Follow me." When I push open the garden gate, Jasper gasps. We walk under the arbor Grampa and I made from old shutters and painted red, though it's now mostly covered in honey-suckle vines.

Jasper runs from one thing to another and stops at the old French horn that Grampa turned into a planter. "I feel like the kids in *Charlie and the Choco-late Factory* when they're first let in."

"I told you. My grampa can fix anything. He says throwing something away is evidence of a lack of imagination, a failure to see what the item's next purpose could be." I point to the teapots of all sizes filled with drooping ferns and our tire-planter garden. "Let me water his plants, and then we can grab the wagons and head out. Mom needs to move the ferns inside before it gets too cold." I mist the autumn sage while Jaspers checks out all the repurposed wonders hidden in Grampa's yard.

"These little candleholders are made out of wine glasses," Jasper yells over.

"I know. Grampa and I found a whole crate of them with only the bases broken. So, we shoved what was left of the stems in the ground, and the bowl is the perfect size for a votive candle." I finish up and wrap the hose back around the hanger that's actually a tire rim I spray-painted bright orange and Grampa mounted to the wall.

"Come on," I yell to Jasper, and he follows me to Grampa's shed. There's an impressive array of supplies inside.

Jasper looks over my shoulder and whispers, "It just keeps getting better."

"I wish I could take you inside Grampa's house. It's like the very best museum. But we don't have time today." I roll out the extra wagon and attach it to

Jasper's bike the same way I did mine the last time. "You can't take turns too fast, or the wagon could swing into your back wheel. But as long as you take it slow, you'll be fine."

I fidget with bungee cords to make sure they're secure. I'm hoping since we're going during the day the security guards will be too busy to give us any trouble.

"Ready?" Jasper asks.

"Ready." I nod and lead the way.

We pass North Lake and the volleyball courts and head toward the highway. To avoid traffic, I take a slow turn onto Hillside Drive and pull into the back of an enormous parking lot. The dumpsters for Electric Ave., the mall's biggest electronics store, are tucked behind a six-foot wall of fencing to block them from view. Hidden treasures.

I scan the parking lot. No "Private Property" signs. No security guards. It's busy but not too bad. I nod toward the fence. "This is good. People are less likely to see us."

Jasper nods. "Let the hunt begin."

I roll my eyes and laugh. There are three

dumpsters and two are already propped open. I point to one swarming with flies. "That one is most likely for the restaurants at the food court. So, steer clear."

This time we brought both Grampa's fancy picking tools. I take out two milk crates for us to stand on. Jasper smiles. "I get to dig this time and not just be a lookout?"

"With these fences the only thing we really need to keep an eye on are those doors." I nod toward a small set of concrete stairs and two metal doors on the brick wall we're facing. One is propped open, revealing a long empty hallway. "Why would they have a door open? Maybe we should come back another day."

Jasper shrugs. "But with the door open, we'll be able to see or hear someone coming. If it's closed, we wouldn't know until they opened it. So, really isn't it better that it's open?"

"Good point."

We slide on the plastic gloves and get to work. But just as Jasper steps up on the crate something nags at me. He doesn't know all the details.

"Wait," I say. "There was some reason Grampa

wouldn't come here. I don't know what it was, and I won't blame you if you want to back out. I should have told you sooner."

"But it's not like we're stealing. They're throwing all this away, right?" Jasper asks.

"As far as I know. Grampa always says once it's out on the curb or in a dumpster, it's fair game. But like I said, it's okay if you want to leave." I step up on my crate so that I'm standing next to him, and hope with my whole heart that he stays.

"It's too late to back out now." Jasper reaches in and grabs a bag with the picking tool, and I do the same. Mine is stuffed full but not too heavy to lower to the pavement on my own. As soon as I pull open the top, video games spill out.

"Jackpot," Jasper whispers.

"They're preowned, but Frank doesn't care. I think I can put the whole bag in the wagon. What's in yours?" I ask.

Jasper carefully unties the knot at the top. "Whoa. Unopened boxes of headphones." He pulls out one box after another of new gaming headsets with microphones. "Six of them in total."

I look the brand up on my phone. "Thirty-five dollars on Amazon." We both start to giggle. "What else?"

"I've got a few off-brand Xbox controllers. And the whole bottom of the bag is full of still-in-the-package adapters, like cords and stuff." Jasper looks up at me with his giant smile. "This is so fun!" His voice gets louder with each word.

"SHHHH." But I laugh also. "Ready for round two?"

Jasper nods. I hook into a bag but can't quite raise it. "Help me with this one. It's too heavy." Jasper uses the pole of his tool to support the bottom of the bag, and once we have it up to the edge, he grabs it and places it beside the wagon. My heart is pounding. A bag that weighs this much must be full of something good.

I rip open the top. Inside are two Nintendo Wiis and new Wii charging stations, preowned but all still in the original packaging.

"Oh man," Jasper whispers. "Is anyone still playing Wii?"

I shrug. "I don't know, but maybe Frank won't know either."

We're so focused on the bag that the metal door slamming closed takes us both by surprise. Luckily, we're already crouched down and hidden from view by the dumpster, and with the lid open like it is, so are our bikes. At first, I'm frozen, but when I hear footsteps on the stairs, I creep forward and start fastening down the bungee net over Jasper's wagon.

"Get on your bike and take off," I whisper. "I'll be right behind you."

Jasper crawls over to his bike and gets on, just as I grab the garbage bag, tie it closed with shaking fingers, and toss it in my wagon.

"Hey!" someone yells. "Those receptacles are private property!"

No time to secure my finds. "Go!" I yell at Jasper, and we take off.

I look back to see a security guard toss a cigarette and get on his radio. Now with the door closed, I see the sign—PRIVATE PROPERTY.

It's impossible to go full speed with the wagons attached. "Let's cut through the park." I veer off Windsor Drive onto the road that leads to a parking lot for North Lake Recreation Center. There's a hiking trail that goes to the fishing pond or up to the recycling center. I make the turn a little too quick. The wagon swings inward and hits my back wheel.

For a moment I'm airborne, and all I'm thinking about is whether all our finds flew out of my wagon. I land on my back. Jasper is screaming my name from the trail. There's this horrible sound, kind of like the cry of a kitten. That's when I realize I can't breathe, and the sound is coming from me struggling to inhale, and just then pain flares in my chest.

Jasper runs over to me. He pulls me up so that I'm sitting, then moves my legs until my knees are bent in front of my chest. "You've had the wind knocked out of you. It happened to me in a soccer game once."

After a few seconds of gasping, the noise and the pain stops, and I'm able to take a breath. I feel weak and a little lightheaded, but I'm not hurt.

"Take slow breaths. In through your nose and out through your mouth," Jasper says. I try to get up, but he puts his hand on my shoulder. "You should just sit for a minute. Everything spilled out, but I think it's all fine."

"I'm okay," I say, then get up slowly and walk back to the trail. The items are all undamaged, like Jasper said. When I look at everything now, I don't even bother opening my heart to see if anything speaks to it. I touch my pocket where the spider pin still rests, trying to call up the feeling of finding something truly special.

We climb back on our bikes. I know I owe Jasper more of an explanation, but when I turn to him, he holds up a hand. "None of that was okay. Let's just get this stuff back to your grampa's." Then he takes off like he knows the way.

Once we pull into Grampa's driveway, I go to open the garage, but Jasper doesn't follow. He's busy unwrapping the bungee cord connecting his bike to the wagon.

"Not illegal, huh?" he says. "Then why did that guy run after us screaming, and why did we take off like that?"

"I'm sorry," I say. "I should've gone alone."

"Or not at all," Jasper says. "I don't think I can go with you on hunts anymore. Maybe you should stop too."

I gesture to Grampa's house. "I have to fix this whole mess, get Grampa back home, and make everything the way it was."

Jasper climbs back on his bike. "You should take a closer look around here. Your grampa didn't fix all this stuff and get it to work the way it did before. He changed things and made them into something else."

I don't want to think about what he's saying. But I also don't want him to leave still angry at me. "I told you everything I knew. But I should've known that Grampa's reasons for not going there were good ones." I point to our wagons. "All this stuff would've ended up in some landfill, and maybe it's enough to convince my mom that I can make up the difference and cover Grampa's monthly expenses. I couldn't have done it without you. Even if you never talk to me again—thank you."

Jasper scoffs, but I see just the side of his mouth rise a little. "It was sort of exciting." Not a smile but a hint of one. "And you did warn me. And we did find some good stuff, didn't we?"

I nod. "Some great stuff."

He nods too, but says, "I better head home."

"You still want to come to Frank's tomorrow and see what we can get for all this?" I ask.

Jasper shrugs. "Let me think about it." He takes off and says, "See you tomorrow."

I watch his back as he pedals down Grampa's street, hoping he'll look back and give me one of his smiles. He doesn't.

After storing our finds, I get home about an hour before Mom does and manage to make it through dinner with her chatting about her upcoming competition.

Mom is so focused on the National Expo that she blurts out random ideas in the middle of eating. She drops her fork and yells, "Suspenders!" then jumps up to write it down in her inspiration journal. Even though I'm in a tangle over what happened with Jasper, I laugh out loud.

"Don't mock genius." While Mom jots, I check my phone, sigh, and put it down for the hundredth time. "I hope your long face isn't because you're feeling upset over a boy." Mom is staring at me. "Want to talk about whatever happened between you and Jasper?"

"Jasper and I are just friends." At least, I hope we're still friends.

"Jasper's a nice kid." Mom reaches over and squeezes my hand. "True friends can work things out."

Right as I'm about to go to bed, my phone buzzes. It's a text from Jasper. Sorry. Can't go tomorrow.

18

MONDAY MORNING, THE TIGHTNESS IN MY THROAT is back with a vengeance. I can't quit thinking about Jasper's text. He's definitely still mad at me.

I've never dreaded riding the bus as much as I do when I round the corner onto Cedar Street. But Ashley is standing alone. She smiles and says, "Hey, Mabel."

"Hey." I look down Magnolia Drive. "Where's Farrah?"

"Her aunt had her twins early. And since we have Friday off school this week, Farrah and her mom went to visit."

All I say is "Oh."

When the bus pulls up, we get on together. Ashley walks to the fourth row on the left and stops so that I can get into my old seat. I pause and she sort of shrugs and says, "I know things have been weird. But we're still friends, right?"

"Right," I say, but I'm really not sure. I step in and sit by the window. Ashley settles in next to me and bumps my shoulder with hers. At first, it feels so familiar, like I've managed to jump back in time to when things were less complicated. But then McKenna gets on. She's carrying the cardboard box for our Rube Goldberg machine and has already attached a few of the train tracks to make our inclined plane.

"Hey," I say when she gets to our row. "I have everything we need in my bag."

McKenna nods and says, "I really hope the pulley works."

"Me too," I say, and McKenna gives me a little wave as she walks past.

Ashley looks back to where I've been sitting with McKenna and Jasper. Then she asks, "Do you have a costume for the Fall Festival yet? Since Farrah won't be back in time maybe we could go as something together? Just like old times." The Fall Festival is on Friday, we have that day off school, and Halloween is on Sunday. A weekend Halloween is like a magical alignment of the planets.

"What about the rock star thing?" I ask.

Ashley shrugs. "With Farrah gone it doesn't make sense. So, I'd rather do something with you, if you want."

"Well, I have a few ideas. I was going to wear all my rain gear and attach stuffed cats and dogs to my umbrella. But maybe we could think of something together. Like a needle and a haystack. Or I could wear a big cardboard box and you could be a think bubble. Think outside the box."

Ashley laughs and wrinkles her nose. "I don't know. Will anyone know what we are?"

I laugh too and shrug.

Ashley folds her arms and sighs. "Maybe we shouldn't even dress up. We're getting kind of old for it."

I gasp. "What? No way."

"Okay. Well, we better come up with something quick."

We sit together and think. Just the two of us. Just like old times.

"What if we wear our costumes from last year? Anne and Diana."

Is she saying we're best friends again? My spider pin has been demoted to my backpack's pocket and it sparkles up at me from the bus floor. If Farrah were here, would Ashley even be talking to me? Probably not, but Farrah isn't here. Being left out feels awful, and even though Ashley might deserve it, I don't want to do that to her. Surely a friendship deserves as much of a chance to be salvaged as anything else. So, I say, "Okay."

At Jasper's stop it takes all my energy not to look at him. When I glance up, he keeps his eyes forward. I focus on Ashley while she tells me all about her dad's new house. Once we get to school, I rush to get off the bus before Jasper and try to ignore how badly I wish he would have at least said hi.

Mrs. Kirkpatrick's room is bustling. Our energy,

forces, and motion unit ended and projects are due today. Partners gather around desks unpacking all their materials. McKenna hops in place. "I can't wait to see it," she says as soon as I put my backpack down. We've been planning for weeks and broken our machine into parts, each handling different tasks. I've sent her a photo of our Rube Goldberg showstopper, but she hasn't seen it in person.

I unzip my bag and pull out the mannequin head Grampa and I found outside Pearle Vision a while back. He has a little paint chipping around the bridge of his nose, where most likely display glasses sat for years, but he's otherwise in great condition.

"He's perfect," McKenna says, and she starts taking out the supplies from her bag. McKenna's cut a wire hanger in the middle, then taken the wire and slid it through the hole in the center of an empty spool of thread. "And here's our fixed pulley."

We remove the top flaps of the cardboard container and sit it on its side to create a sort of shadow box, then we attach the hanger to the top. McKenna ties one end of a thin rope to a plastic strawberry basket and laces the rope over the spool. I hot-glue the other end to the top button of an Oklahoma City Thunder ballcap. The basket hangs on one side of the pulley, and below, the hat sits on the mannequin head. We run a golf ball down a series of inclined planes built with wooden train tracks. At the last track the ball falls through a plastic cup with no bottom, into the basket, and lifts the hat off the mannequin.

Mrs. Kirkpatrick walks around inspecting everyone's progress. "A few more minutes for trial runs, and then we'll have our first presenters," she calls. She stops by our table and nods slowly. "Very nice work, you two. Extra points for unique materials, but you need a title. What's your machine called?"

McKenna looks at me wide-eyed. How could we forget a title?

"Hmm. How about the De-cap-tivator?" I ask.

Mrs. Kirkpatrick laughs and says, "I'd say that's perfect, and very Rube Goldberg of you." As Mrs. Kirkpatrick walks off, McKenna gives me a big hug and I hug her back. I replay our machine and that hug for the rest of my morning classes, and all my thoughts stay positive.

Jasper and I aren't in the same classes, so I don't

see him again until lunch. Ashley waits with me in line, even though she's brought her own. David Verdon walks past and says "Hey" in Ashley's general direction.

"Hey," Ashley says. She waits until he goes to sit down, then she sort of buries her face in my shirt sleeve and giggles. "I can't believe he said hi. *And* while I'm in the school lunch line."

I stare down at my tray. "What's wrong with the lunch line?" Today is chicken fingers with tater tots, only bested by pizza Fridays.

Ashley shrugs. "Nothing. It's just some kids are saying only poor kids eat school lunch. But that's not what I think."

We walk toward our old table. "Right. Especially since a month ago you were eating school lunch too. Besides, you love the chicken fingers."

"Exactly," Ashley says. "Sorry."

We sit down and Ashley stares at my tray. I sigh and pass her one of the chicken fingers. She laughs her wild, snorty laugh then covers her nose. And for a second, I forget about the school lunch comment.

"How's your grampa doing?" she asks between bites.

"Okay, I guess. He's getting better and is able to walk with a cane now."

"At least you don't have to go on more dumpster dives, huh?" Ashley asks.

A piece of paper lands on the table. It's a folded note. As Ashley unfolds it, her eyes widen. Her face is turning splotchy, but I can't tell if that's good or bad anymore. She slides the note toward me.

"David thinks you're cute," is written in squashed print.

I laugh. "Well, that's way more embarrassing than eating school lunch."

Ashley reaches across and snatches the note out of my hands. "Maybe he's my Gilbert Blythe. Besides, I think he's nice." Gilbert is Anne's one true love in *Anne of Green Gables*. They start off on the wrong foot and he's sort of annoying in the beginning, but David is so much worse.

I snort. "You're joking, right?" Ashley glares at me. Okay, not joking, but *nice*? David spits loogies on the sidewalk. There is a whole collection of boogers wiped under the aisle-side seat on the tenth row of our bus and every single one of them is from his nose. And he called me fat all through third grade. I think of jokes that I could've said to Ashley before this summer.

He's snot the one.

Could there be a worse boy to pick?

Who's better than David Verdon? Everyboogie.

Ashley puts the note in her lunch box. "I knew you wouldn't understand," she mumbles.

"You're right. I don't get it." I point over to his table. He has a Cheeto shoved up each nostril. I want to say that I don't understand liking Farrah either. But I just stare down at my remaining chicken fingers.

Ashley turns back to me and sighs. "Maybe you have a point." She bites into her sandwich, and we spend the rest of lunch eating. There's something uncomfortable about the quiet. Maybe it's because I have things I want to say but can't. Or maybe it's because I do have things to say, just not to her anymore.

I spend the rest of the time staring around the lunchroom. Mrs. Brandon, the lunch lady, smiles at every kid in line. Jasper sits clear across the room and talks much louder than I'd realized. He's giving McKenna one of his giant grins while she gestures wildly. They look happy. David sits at table 6 and does not limit his nose picking to the bus.

"Saturday you can come over to Dad's and swim. The pool is heated," Ashley says.

"That'd be fun." Or maybe it'll be full of more uncomfortable quiets.

On the bus ride home, Ashley talks the whole way about her dad's new neighborhood and the puppy he's promised her. A few blocks from Whispering Pines, Jasper gets off and walks down the block without looking back. I tell Ashley about Mom's almost-winning table and she even does her snort laugh a few more times without trying to cover it up. When we get off the bus, she gives me a quick hug like we always used to do.

I don't know what I was thinking at lunch; it's good to be back in the fourth row. But then I see McKenna walking toward her house alone and think of Jasper at Whispering Pines, and I worry I'm making a mistake. Ashley's been pretty terrible to me lately, and Jasper and McKenna never have. But I'm not even sure Jasper and I are friends anymore.

I distract myself by going over my trash-to-cash

plan as I walk. I'll go home, bike to Grampa's, and then head over to Frank's. With or without Jasper, I still need to prove I can make money each month. And I only have an hour before Mom will get home from work.

I rush into the house, only to find Mom already there.

"Hey, what are you doing home so early?" I ask. Looks like Frank's will have to wait.

"Nice to see you too," Mom says. She wraps me in an unexpected hug. "Did you have a good day?" I nod and Mom ruffles my hair like Grampa always does.

The dining table is covered with bags of rhinestones, strips of black pleather, and rolls of red ribbon. I point to a glove coated in silver glitter. "What's all this?"

"Oh, I took the afternoon off to work on these. I volunteered to make centerpieces for the Halloween show at Whispering Pines as a favor to Margaret. I think I'll have the glove rising out of an arrangement of red roses. They're going to be small, but a dozen is still a big job. Plus, the whole "Thriller" song happens in a graveyard, and I imagine that's the last place most of the residents want to think of. But Margaret is counting on me and so is Pattie. Each vase has to have a Pattie's Parties business card."

"Ah, right. Grampa mentioned the party." I push the memory of Jasper being there out of my head. "Who's Margaret? And why a glove?"

Mom scrunches her eyes up at me. "Michael Jackson wore one sparkly glove. It was his thing. And Margaret is Mrs. Hayden, the social director."

I nod.

"Enough about me and Michael Jackson. Tell me about your day." She tosses one of the gloves at me.

Mom always has advice for me instead of just listening like Grampa does. I don't know if it was the hug/hair-ruffle combo, or that she used vintage glass on her table, but today I tell her about Farrah and how I was afraid Ashley might not want to be friends anymore. This time Mom listens, and when I'm done talking, she says, "I don't understand why you all can't be friends."

"Maybe we can," I say. Mom gets up and kisses me on the head. I already feel a ton better. I guess being loved on a little and listened to was all I needed.

"Well, if you want to wear that costume, it'll need some alterations." When mom first started pageanting, she learned to sew. She's good too, but she usually doesn't have time. "Let's get it out and see if we can't add a little more spiff to it," she says. "I have extra lace somewhere." She starts off down the hall. "And a straw hat! Oh, I know—a pinafore!"

The whole dining room quickly fills with her supplies—thread, boxes of fabric, a dressmaking dummy, and her sewing machine.

"I almost forgot," Mom says as she grabs her handbag, pulls out an envelope, and slides it toward me.

Inside are two tickets. I pull them out and see the words *Collector's Menagerie* printed across the top and almost drop them.

Mom smiles. "Out of thirty thousand applicants only twelve thousand got tickets. Let's hope it's the beginning of our winning streak. There's more information about bringing in an item to be appraised."

I tuck the tickets back inside the envelope. All I can think of is Grampa not being able to go.

"You look shocked." Mom laughs. "I knew you'd be excited."

I nod and try to squeeze out a smile.

Mom gestures to the costume on the table. "Well, try it on." Her eyes widen. "Let's add a ruffle at the bottom. And a whole white cotton and lace pinafore to wear over it?"

I groan and put on the dress.

"Okay, okay. No lace." Mom laughs.

Maybe it's Mom mentioning ruffles, but poor Edna Worn from *Collector's Menagerie* with her painted table pops into my head. She'd only wanted to make it look beautiful and ended up decreasing its value. And I start wondering about all the people on *Collector's Menagerie* who think they have something special and then find out they were wrong all along.

Mom pauses. "Remember the year Ashley desperately wanted to be Belle and wanted you to be the Beast? First grade, I think." She looks at me and her smile widens. She touches her pearls with one hand and my cheek with the other. "You're a good friend, and I hope you know you're Ashley's equal, not her shadow. She's been lucky to have you." She stands back to look at me. "I'll work on the pinafore, but we need to head over to Grampa's before it gets too late."

Mom is just being Mom, but there's something about what she said that bothers me. I keep trying to figure it out while we drive to Whispering Pines.

As we park, I still I have this sort of sticky, not-quite-right feeling. People only say things are like old times when things aren't like old times anymore. *Ashley's been lucky to have me.* Been. Past tense. Over and done. Plus, Mom called Whispering Pines "Grampa's" like she's already said goodbye to his house.

Ashley wants me to not like treasure hunting, to like David Verdon, and be like boring, loyal Diana. Maybe my friendship with Ashley isn't as special as I thought. Maybe it's not worth what I thought it was. Maybe not to her, anyways.

Dinner with Grampa that night reminds me of my lunch with Ashley. There's all this stuff I want to say but can't. I can't tell him about the haul Jasper and I made. I can't tell him about the tickets Mom got to *Collector's Menagerie.* And I can't tell him how badly I miss him and all the things we used to do together. Then what Ray Reno said to Edna about her table crosses my mind, how some things are so changed they can't ever be brought back to what they once were.

"Everything okay, Mae-mae?" Grampa asks.

"Everything's fine." I give him my best impression of a real smile and hope that he's not so great at spotting a fake.

19

TUESDAY MORNING, WHEN THE BUS PASSES THE little playground Ashley and I used to meet at almost every day of summer vacation, I say, "Remember when we pretended the slide was our boat and we were floating in the Barry family's pond just like Anne does?"

Ashley looks over at the slide. "I can't believe all the embarrassing stuff we used to do."

I didn't think it was embarrassing. In fact, I'd do it again tomorrow. But instead I say, "Yeah."

I make it through the morning, and at lunch while I'm in line Jasper stops by.

"Hey," he says. He glances over at Ashley. "So, did you go by Frank's yesterday?"

"Couldn't. Mom was home." I want to ask him to go with me today, but I can't. Not in front of Ashley. Plus, he might say no. "I'm going to swing by there today and then go see Archie on the way home."

He nods. "Cool. Well, see you later." As he walks toward table 4, he waves.

"Are you sure he's not your 'good friend'?" Ashley asks, and then laughs.

"I'm sure." I take my hamburger from Mrs. Brandon and make a point of saying thank you and returning her smile.

I eat while Ashley looks over her shoulder, waves at David, then giggles when he waves back. Honestly, I'm so disgusted that it's difficult to eat.

All Ashley wants to talk about during lunch and on the entire bus ride home is David Verdon. Once I'm inside the apartment, I'm almost relieved not to have to listen to her for a while. I text Mom just to check in but also to be sure she's working all afternoon. I ask if I can bike over to the Tuesday Thrift and cross my fingers until her response comes back.

Sure, but be careful. It's only a tiny lie. I *am* going to try to swing by Archie's. But now I have plenty of time to bike to Grampa's, load everything into one wagon, head to Frank's, and hopefully say hi to Archie on the way home. Also, I need to see if any of the baby merchandise sold.

Frank owns Frank's Pawn and Salvage and smokes an old corncob pipe, and the tobacco, while horrible for his health, smells sweet and woodsy. I walk in, take a deep breath, and pause by the wall of electric guitars. I browse for a minute, for the first time in a while listening to see if anything calls to my heart.

As soon as he sees me, Frank abandons his word search puzzle and stands up. We're not the hugging type of friends, so he gives me a single nod and reaches out for a handshake. "Mabel, I was so sorry to hear about your grampa. I gave him a call last week and we chatted for a while."

"He's getting better every day," I say.

"That's exactly what he said." Frank laughs and

then looks around me to the wagon I have piled high and parked outside. "What do you have for me?" It's just like Frank to get right to business.

He follows me outside and starts riffling through my finds. "I'm not gonna lie to you. I have a hard time moving preowned games. But the headsets and the game consoles look great." Frank pulls out his phone and does some price checks. "Hmm. I'll give you two twenty-five for everything."

"Two hundred and twenty-five dollars?"

Frank nods. I almost go ahead and give him a hug, but instead I jump up and down.

"Sounds good, I guess?" Frank laughs again. "Follow me and we'll get you settled."

Once the bills are in my hand, it's not the tall stack I imagined, but still more money than I've ever held. When I slide the money into the small pocket on my backpack, I see the spider pin and decide to whisper, "Thank you," maybe to the spider, maybe to Frank, or maybe just to the universe.

"See you soon, Frank. And thanks for doing business with me," I say.

"No problem, kid. You get another load like that, bring it by anytime." He goes back to work on his word search puzzle.

I ride to Archie's with an empty wagon, but a backpack stuffed with cash and high hopes.

As soon as I turn into the parking lot, I see a familiar bike parked in front of the Tuesday Thrift. Archie gets up from his usual spot behind the register, and after he surrounds me with one of his signature hugs, he whispers, "He's in aisle ten. Been waiting there for almost an hour." Then he slides me two twenty-dollar bills. "Three plush pigs, a few onesies, and the bouncer all sold today."

"Thanks, Archie." I hug him back and he manages to slip butterscotch candies into my hand.

For the first time I don't go straight to glassware, but to the back, lined with bookshelves. Jasper has three stacks on the floor and sits cross-legged with a book open on his lap and a butterscotch bulging under one cheek.

"Careful or you'll be buried in a book avalanche," I say.

Jasper looks up and smiles. "Hey, I had to know

what happened at Frank's and I remembered you said you were stopping by here."

"Two. Hundred. Twenty. Five. Dollars," I whisper. "Plus, forty more from Archie."

"What?" Jasper's eyes are wide.

I unzip the small pocket of my bag. "I want you to have half." I start counting out the money, but Jasper puts his hand on mine.

"I won't take it," he says.

"Will you at least let me buy you a milkshake and some fries?"

Jasper laughs. "It's hard to say no to fries."

"And this stack of books," I say as I pick up his tallest tower. He starts to protest. I want to tell Jasper that I've missed him even though it's only been a few days. Actually, I want to give him a huge hug too.

"It's even harder for me to turn down books," he says.

"I know. Come on."

Jasper and I walk to the register. Archie rings us up and asks, "Any heart finds lately?"

"Not today," I say, like always. Jasper shakes his head as he puts his new books in his backpack.

Archie frowns but then brightens. "You know, your mom gave me a story. Wrote it down just the other day."

"My mom?" I'm shocked. "My mom doesn't have a heart find."

"She was dropping off some of your grampa's stuff and told me the story of her pearl necklace. Sure sounded like a heart find to me," he says.

"Wait. She was dropping off what of Grampa's?" I ask.

Archie shrugs. "Haven't gone through the boxes yet. She said he's finally decided to let her go through some of his things. And it's about time."

Suddenly my throat tightens, and I'm not sure why. I thank Archie again and walk out with Jasper.

"You okay?" Jasper asks as we walk two doors over to the diner.

"It's just unusual for Grampa to get rid of things. It's unusual for Mom to stop by Archie's. And it's even more unusual that neither of them mentioned it. Grampa never keeps secrets from me." We walk toward the same booth we sat in last time. "About keeping secrets, I'm really sorry about the mall."

"I would've gone anyway, but if you'd told me the whole story, I could have made the choice to go. I think that's what upset me." Jasper sighs as we slide into opposite sides of a booth. "My parents didn't tell me my dad had lost his job for almost a month. Things were strange for the longest time, and I didn't know why. When they finally told me what was going on, I was relieved almost, just to know the truth."

"Wow," I say.

Jasper nods. "I mean, they talked me through everything, tried to make sure I understood, and told me what to expect with Grandma. Mom seems happier now that she can talk to me about it a little. And Dad's even interviewed for a few jobs here. But still I wish they'd been honest with me from the start."

I say the only thing I can think of. "Well, I'm glad you're here."

"Sometimes, I am too." Jasper laughs. "You know what I like best about your and Archie's heart-find idea? The story part. That things aren't just things, but sometimes they're a story, something that their owner believes in. Does that make sense?"

I nod again. We place our order, and after the

waitress leaves, Jasper cocks his head and looks at me. "You have one, don't you?"

"Have one what?"

"Come on, Mabel. Archie already said you have a notebook. It can't just be full of other people's finds." Jasper waits before saying, "So, I have one. Well, a whole collection really. You know those Little Golden Books? Well, I have most of Mom's from when she was a kid. The stories aren't all that great, but each one has my mother's name written in wobbly crayon from when she was little and then my name is under hers. I don't know why, but sometimes I can flip to that 'This book belongs to' page, and I feel better."

"That's why Grampa and I love collecting so much. And there are some objects that are extra special."

Jasper crosses his arms and waits again.

"Okay, okay. I have this little glass basket. It's sort of red swirled with yellow. Grampa and I found it at Archie's a few years ago. It's really pretty, except for a little chip in the handle. Grampa talked me into buying it, not because it was perfect, but because it was one of a kind." Like me, is what Grampa would say if he were here.

"Like you," Jasper says, and gives me one of his mega smiles.

I wave him off and feel my cheeks burning.

"Speaking of one of a kinds, have you come up with your completely original costume idea yet?"

"So, about that...Ashley is probably going to meet up with us too. At the Fall Festival on Friday. And then maybe we could all go trick-or-treating together on Sunday?" Why not? If Ashley can be friends with me and Farrah, why can't I be friends with her and Jasper and McKenna too?

Jasper stares at me for what feels like forever before he says, "Okay."

Our order arrives and he immediately takes a long drink of his milkshake then shudders.

"We've been friends since we were babies." I take a burning hot fry and grab the ketchup. "She's nice."

"Really?" Jasper asks.

"Well, she used to be nice when she was my best friend." I try to joke, but it's too close to the truth to laugh.

"Back in Chicago, I didn't have many friends my own age. I love to read for lots of reasons, but one is if my head is in a book then kids are less likely to mess with me. Sort of like a shield, I guess." Jasper stares out the window for a minute. "Anyways, I think friends should be like bowler hats. And make you feel bigger inside."

I nod and think over what Jasper just said about friendship. When I picture myself in that Diana Barry costume, I sure don't feel bigger inside.

Before we leave, I ask, "Are you sure you won't let me give you half the money?"

"Nope." He steps onto his bike. "Every Tuesday let's meet here, and then I'll let you buy me a shake and fries after. Eventually, you'll pay me back."

"Deal," I say. This time Jasper smiles and waves before he turns onto Cedar Drive.

Once I swing by Grampa's, drop off the wagon, and bike home, the sun is sinking and Mom's car is already in the parking lot.

She's unloading groceries in the kitchen. "Hey, you're getting home kind of late," she says.

"Jasper met me at the Tuesday Thrift." I leave out Frank's and the milkshakes and french fries.

Mom looks at all the groceries, then at me. "Hey, what do you say we have dinner with Grampa tonight. After work, grocery shopping, and putting everything away, I don't really feel like cooking."

"Sounds good to me," I say.

Mom grabs her bag, and we swing by Sonic for takeout and then head to Whispering Pines. The front desk nurse tells us Grampa's in the back garden.

"I didn't even know there was a garden," I say to Mom.

"I told you it was nice," she says. I roll my eyes as hard as possible. She laughs and we walk through the first floor to a set of double doors and out into a garden with a few raised beds and outdoor furniture sprinkled in clusters on a paved patio. Grampa sits at a table with Mr. Curtis, Toni, and Mrs. Wingfield. He's peering over a small fan of cards, plays his hand, and the whole table erupts with laughter, except for Mrs. Wingfield.

When Grampa sees us his face breaks into an even bigger smile. "There's my girl. Winning at Penny Poker and having dinner with my two favorite people as the sun sets? I don't know if this day can get any better."

Toni bumps Mrs. Wingfield gently and says, "Oh, Helen, lighten up. Bobby won fair and square."

But Mrs. Wingfield is stone faced; she points at Grampa. "I don't know about fair, but he's a square all right."

Mom's eyes go wide, she leans over and whispers, "Square is an old insult; it means boring." The rest of the table is quiet for a second, before they all crack up again and Mrs. Wingfield manages a little grin.

We end up at a table in the cafeteria with Grampa. Mr. Curtis brings his tray over and sits with us and so does Toni. It's a rowdy dinner full of loud laughter and bad jokes. Mom and I even stay and watch some show about Navy detectives. Seeing Grampa with all his new friends makes me feel hopeful that things might work out with mine.

By the time we get back to the Cascades it's dark. Mom yawns and points to her purse on the floorboard beneath my legs. "Would you mind grabbing my bag?"

My phone buzzes. "I'll be up in just a sec." Mom nods and heads to the stairs. I look at my phone. It's a text from Jasper saying Costume Clue #1 with a photo of a ballpoint pen. I shake my head, grab Mom's bag, and open the door. Mom's purse opens and a few things spill out onto my seat. Mixed with the lipsticks and a tiny package of tissues are three business cards, all for real estate agents.

Mom wasn't just getting rid of a few of Grampa's things. She's selling his house.

20

FOR TWO WHOLE DAYS, THE ABOUT-TO-CRY KNOT never completely goes away. In fact, now it's even larger and rock solid, like one of Grampa's shooter marbles. It's there when I go to sleep and back first thing in the morning. By Friday, I'm almost used it, like that achy hard feeling is now a part of me.

I haven't said anything about the real estate cards. I don't know where to start. And I can't believe I thought that just because Mom included some old dessert bowls in her table that she'd actually listen to me. If she's talked to real estate agents, then she's already made up her mind about selling Grampa's house. And that means Grampa must have agreed to it. I've sorted through the details and the maybes over and over, and the thing that upsets me most is they made these decisions without talking to me at all.

Since there isn't school, I stay in bed late. The smell of mom's coffee wafts down the hall, followed by Mom. She knocks gently and comes in, even though I don't answer. Her rollers are the size of tin cans; this is how she gets her "beach waves." Looking at her causes the same feeling that I got when Ashley said only poor kids eat school lunch. Finally, I understand that it's anger, but a deep, quiet kind that's new to me.

"Hey, instead of spending the whole day watching TV, why don't you swing by Pattie's and have lunch with me?"

I want to say no. But I can't think of an excuse. "Fine."

"Fine?" Mom puts a hand on her hip.

"Yes. Sounds great. Can't wait." I roll over and face my window. The sky is overcast. No light shines through my Amberina basket.

"Okay." I feel questions coming, but instead she

says, "Well, I'm running late. So, I'll see you around noon?"

"Bye." I don't roll back to face her, and I don't get up until I hear the front door close. When I'm pouring my bowl of cereal, my phone buzzes. Another text from Jasper. Costume Clue #2 is a picture of black high tops and a hoodie. Even though I don't feel like responding, I do. So, you're going as you?

He texts right back. My mom says be yourself and you can't go wrong.

I send a smiley face emoji even though I feel like the poop one and turn on the TV. Hours go by and my phone buzzes again. This time it's Mom. Where are you?

I'm still in my pajamas and haven't brushed my teeth, but I text back, On my way.

.⁓⦵⦵⁓.

Pattie's Parties is one of my least favorite places. The candle-scented air, the silk flowers, and most of all, Pattie Pringle. Pattie's floated the possibility of making Mom a partner in the company for years, but so far, all she's done is dangle different opportunities in front of Mom that never seem to happen. At least that's what Grampa says.

As soon as I walk in, Pattie's lips curl up in a forced smile. She scans me head to toe, pausing at my boots for a bit and resting on my hair, before saying, "Your mom's in the back, stocking new table linens. And most likely working more on her mock-up table for tomorrow."

I nod. Pattie doesn't like me to go in the storage room, ever since I broke a glass vase looking for a mark on the bottom. Turns out nothing in Pattie's is marked by an artist because it's all made by machines in a factory. I look around at all the table settings and cases full of silverware and glassware options. Not a single thing is one of a kind. And it's on purpose!

The showroom has three tables: one set for a child's party, one for a wedding, and another for a fortieth birthday. Mom is responsible for all three. She comes up with the concepts, lines up the vendors, places the orders, and makes sure everything is set up the day of the party. All the while, Pattie sits behind the register in front of three big binders. Those binders hold all the party options and pricing information.

The only thing I can tell Pattie is responsible for is taking most of the money.

Mom's in charge of meeting with clients on an appointment basis. Then she spends every weekend she doesn't have a competition working weddings and parties. This very much interferes with her dream of becoming the National Tablescaping Champion. It seems to me Mom already does most of the work.

I sit at the wedding table. The chair is made to look like golden bamboo and has a panel of fabric tied around the back in a cascade as big as a bustle. One lifelike silk rose in the arrangement is slightly bent, as though someone pulled it forward for a sniff.

"Hey, it's almost one o'clock," Mom says as she emerges from the storage room. She squints from the doorway, walks over, and straightens the rose. That's Mom. It's like she can sense when something isn't perfect.

"Sorry. I lost track of time." I'm so tempted to pull the rose back out before we leave, but I resist.

"Well, I've just started something I need to finish up. You'll have to wait a few more minutes." She heads back to the storage room before I can answer.

Pattie just stares at me until Mom comes out again, this time with her purse.

"Ready?" she asks before turning to Pattie. "I got everything on the shelves. I think I might be done for the day if that's all right."

Pattie nods and smiles, showing too many teeth. Mom might not have much practice at spotting a fake, but I do, and everything about Pattie strikes me as forced and a little too perfect to be the real deal.

Maybe the only thing I really like about Mom's job is where it's located. Mom surprises me by heading toward the Icon. I pause just outside the door. We haven't been since Grampa's stroke. Before I can protest, Benny the owner comes out and gives Mom a hug and then turns to me. "I was so sorry to hear about your grampa's stroke and I'm so happy to see you two back here. Anything you like." He extends an open arm inside. "On the house today."

We settle into a different booth, surrounded by pictures of Lady Gaga. I look over at a couple with a little boy sitting in the Princess Diana booth, our regular spot.

"Seems like you're in the kind of mood that can only be made better by a blue plate special," Mom says. I have two impossible things to say to her—I've been treasure hunting in secret, and she can't sell Grampa's house. Icon's blue plate specials are a wonder, but they aren't going to solve this.

Mom takes a deep breath and says, "I can't believe I have a dozen centerpieces to deliver to Whispering Pines tonight and the Expo is tomorrow! And you've got a big night too with the Fall Festival. You excited?"

Not even a little.

I nod. I'm so mad at her it's like the anger is filling up every inch of me, but that visit to Pattie's made me think about how hard she works and how little she complains. It's confusing.

After we eat, we walk past a furniture consignment place that Grampa and I have been to a few times. I look through the plate-glass window and there are the four teak midcentury-modern dining chairs we dropped off in July. Grampa had called them *fan-tast-teak.*

Mom stops at a store called La Di Da. "What do

you say we get something new to wear for tomorrow, like good-luck outfits?" Mom asks.

A good-luck outfit is one being worn when something lucky happens, so by definition, it's not new. But I don't say that. I nod and end up getting talked into a ridiculous orange sweater covered in thick, soft fuzz. The saleslady calls it an eyelash sweater, which taken literally is really disgusting.

Mom is trying on another skirt when she checks her watch and says, "Doesn't the Fall Festival start at five?"

"Yeah, but I can be late." I look down at my Doc Martens. Mom insisted I get the patent leather this year. She said the glossiness made them look like something more than men's work boots. I hate to admit it, but I do like the shine.

"What do you mean? I thought you were going with Ashley. Isn't she just walking over?" Mom asks. "It'd be great to get a picture of you two together like we always do."

I shrug. "She's at her dad's this weekend, so he's dropping her off at the gym. Maybe he can take one when we get there?"

Mom nods. "I can drop you off on my way. I have to get to Whispering Pines early to set up. There's dancing and snacks after and family members can come in costume. Your grampa's really excited. He said Toni is doing his face up like a zombie." Mom says Toni's name all goofy and wiggles her shoulders. "I'll text Jerry and see if they can give you a ride there after the festival." Jerry is Ashley's dad. Maybe Ashley will ask me to stay the night, and we'll make a blanket and pillow fort on their living room floor and watch movies until we fall asleep. All the things we used to do before Farrah.

"Is there something going on with Grampa and Toni?" I ask, already knowing I won't get to stay at Ashley's even if she asked. I'll be up bright and early tomorrow morning, wearing this orange sweater, helping Mom pack the car, and then driving to Tulsa for the competition.

"Well, it's early days, but I think your grampa may have made himself a lady friend." Mom waggles her eyebrows up and down then turns her attention back to the full-length mirror. "If I win, Pattie is

going to give me control of all the wedding arrangements, linens, table settings, chairs—all of it. She's
looking to hand off the business soon, and her son
sure isn't interested."

Sitting there holding the new sweater I don't
want, the news of Grampa having a girlfriend starts
mixing with all my other problems, and I feel like
jumping up and running down Main Street screaming, all the way to Grampa's house. Maybe his garden
might make me feel better. Then I remember that it
won't be Grampa's for long.

Mom spins, letting the skirt flare out around her.
"What do you think? Is this the one?"

"It looks exactly like the three before," I mumble.

"What?" Mom asks.

"It's perfect," I say. It's easier to tell her what she
wants to hear than to say all the stuff building up
inside me.

Mom changes and pays, and we walk back to Pattie's. I load my bike into the trunk. It won't close all
the way, so we take the back roads home.

As soon as we're in the apartment, Mom grabs the

pinafore she's been working on for one last inspection. "Come. Put it on. I still need to trim off a few stray threads."

A pinafore is really just a fancy apron. But Mom's made mine to look just like the one Diana Barry wore in the miniseries. It's pale blue with little flowers. She's also decorated a straw hat with daisies, a matching blue ribbon, and two fake braids. It's so perfect that I feel like we might step out into Avonlea when Mom opens the apartment door. But it's just our parking lot.

I help mom load her supplies for the Halloween tables at Whispering Pines. When I go back in for the last box, I glance over to my backpack. I've not been without my spider pin since Grampa and I found it. But I can't really carry my backpack to the party, and it doesn't quite fit with my Diana Barry outfit, so I leave it.

Once we're in the car, she looks down at my boots. "Those are the shoes you're wearing?"

I nod and change the subject. "So, they're just friends? Grampa and Toni."

Mom shrugs. "He wants us all to have dinner

together sometime. Seems like more than friends to me." Mom looks at me, motions me over, adjusts my hat, and says, "There. You look perfect, if I do say so myself. Ready to go?"

On the ride to school, my costume doesn't feel so magical anymore. I stare at my shiny Docs, the one thing I'm wearing that still feels like me, until we pull to a stop.

21

THERE'S A SMALL CROWD OUTSIDE THE SCHOOL gym when Mom and I pull up. I take out my phone. No text from Ashley or Jasper.

Mom laughs. "Are you going in or what?"

I nod.

"If Jerry can't drop you off, text me when you're ready, and I'll sneak away and come pick you up. Okay?"

As I get out, Mom lowers her window to wave and yell, "Don't forget about that picture."

I wave to Mom and walk past two Jedi and a Miles Morales Spider-Man. There are definitely no other kids wearing a pinafore—at least I've succeeded in being original.

Halloween might be my favorite holiday. Dress up *and* candy? I can't believe Ashley thought about not wearing a costume. But then I see Gwynn Lester in a regular dress and heels. I walk toward the door trying to convince myself that she's the one who looks ridiculous, but my costume is suddenly uncomfortably warm.

I scan the room. Someone with long blue hair that flows past her waist and a purple star painted over one eye crosses the floor. I can't believe it's Ashley until she's standing right in front of me.

"Oh my gosh. I'm so sorry. Dad said he would call your mom and tell her we changed the plan and that you should just wear that other costume you told me about. I left my phone at Mom's house, and he made this big point of making me spend a day without it." She looks back across the gym, and I see a flash of pink hair—Farrah. "Farrah came back early."

"Why didn't *you* use your dad's phone to call?" I mean to ask, but it comes out more like shouting.

"Your number is stored in my phone. I don't have it memorized." Ashley is looking right at me. "I said

I was sorry." Her eyes don't say sorry. They say just get over it and don't embarrass me. Again.

I point over at Farrah. "You had my mom's number! You couldn't call me, but you worked all this out with her?" Ashley has that red splotchy look again. Now I'm definitely yelling, and Mr. Thatcher, our gym teacher, starts walking over. "Why don't you just come out and say it. You only asked me to do something with you because Farrah wasn't around and you're afraid of being alone. You don't want to be friends anymore, and you're too much of a coward to tell me. Maybe you're just hoping that if you treat me like garbage long enough, I'll figure it out. Well, guess what? I understand!" I tear the hat off my head. "Also, Anne Shirley is ridiculous and vain for most of the first book!"

I feel a hand on my arm. "Hey, you came! I didn't know if you'd show up or not." It's Jasper. He's wearing a black hoodie over an orange T-shirt with jeans and black Converse high tops. "Come on. Let's go." He gently pulls me toward a group of kids gathered around the snack table.

"I think I just want to go home," I mumble.

Actually, I really want to throw my hat and pinafore in the trash and run all the way back to Grampa's house.

"Don't leave unless you want to. But definitely pretend to have a good time for a little bit before you go." Jasper checks his phone. "My mom is leaving for the show at Whispering Pines soon. Want to just catch a ride with her?"

I nod. "Let me make sure it's okay with my mom." I text and get the thumbs-up emoji. Then I spend the longest ten minutes ever meeting all of Jasper and McKenna's friends from science club. McKenna is wearing a lab coat and a gray mustache, and has her hair sprayed silver and standing on end.

I smile when I see her. "Einstein?"

She nods. Her hair doesn't even wobble. "But I think this amount of hair spray is affecting my vision and sense of smell."

McKenna and Jasper laugh, and I'm surprised when I do too. But then Ashley joins David Verdon on the dance floor. They're not really dancing. He's doing some wave motion with his arms, and Ashley is sort of swaying and laughing even though it isn't funny.

Jasper nudges me. "Mom's outside. Ready?"

I nod, and when we walk out, I don't look back.

The inside of Jasper's van isn't like our car. The back-seat pockets are bulging with clipboards and art supplies and books. This ride would give Mom hives.

"Excuse the mess," Amanda says as we climb in the back. Jasper sits with me even though the front is empty.

I shrug out of the pinafore and toss the hat on the seat.

"So, Anne of Green Gables, huh?" Jasper asks.

I cross my arms. "I don't really want to talk about it. Besides, you didn't even wear a costume."

Jasper grabs his chest like he's offended. "Excuse me." I notice his shirt has a silhouette of Medusa, the Camp Half-Blood insignia. He pulls out a ballpoint pen and clicks it, and I finally get it.

"Ah, you're Percy Jackson!"

"Bingo," Jasper says. He shakes his head. "I had no idea you were an Anne of Green Gables fan."

"Actually, I'm supposed to be Diana Barry." Not that this explanation makes it any better.

Jasper's brow crinkles. "Who?"

"I think you look nice," Amanda interrupts and

sends Jasper a look in the rearview mirror. "We're in for a treat tonight. I saw the rehearsal today and the residents are so excited." Her eyes flick to me in the mirror again. "Your grampa is a great guy, and your mom is a real character too. I've really enjoyed getting to know them both." Amanda gives me a big smile exactly like Jasper's.

I make an effort to return the smile. "Can I ask you a question about therapy?"

Amanda nods.

"How much does it cost once Grampa isn't in Whispering Pines?"

"Well, it depends. Your grampa will need occupational therapy, physical therapy, and speech therapy for a while. Right now, he has OT, PT, and Speech once a week."

"And how much does a session cost?" I ask.

"Well, different places charge slightly different amounts, but most sessions run thirty to forty-five minutes. The cost can vary from around one to several hundred dollars. Insurance coverage varies also."

I only understand about half of what she's said. But one thing's for sure, it sounds like a lot of money.

"Have you talked to your mom about all this? She'd have a better idea of what your grampa's situation looks like."

I nod, though it isn't really true. Then I stare out the window until I feel a slight pressure on my wrist. It's Jasper, and he gives my hand a little squeeze before letting go.

22

THE WHISPERING PINES SOCIAL ROOM IS FULL of round tables, each one draped in dark green crushed velvet so plush it looks like grass. Clear glass vases are wrapped in a wide red ribbon, and the rims are dripping with moss. Red roses and twigs rise up in various heights, looking both spooky and beautiful. Sticking out from under each vase is a single sequined glove, reminding me of the witch's shoes poking out from under Dorothy's house in *The Wizard of Oz*. I have to admit, Mom did a great job.

Mom walks over holding bags of glass jewels. "Amanda, thank you so much for giving Mabel a ride."

"My pleasure." Amanda looks around the room. "These tables are amazing."

Mom waves a hand and pretends to be embarrassed, then turns to me and Jasper. "I could sure use some help, if you two are free."

She holds out three Ziploc baggies filled with small, medium, and large rhinestones. "I need a handful of each of these tossed around the base of the vases, varying the placement and size so not too much of the same are grouped together. Think dew drops on blades of grass."

Jasper salutes and gets to work. Mom laughs, then she pauses and looks me over. "Where's the rest of your costume?"

"Oh, I must have left it in Amanda's car."

Part of me wishes Mom would wrap her arms around me and ask me what happened, but instead she says, "I worked hard on those, you know. We'll talk later, okay? I really need to focus right now. KTEN News is doing a feel-good piece on this performance. Pattie donated all the supplies, so I have to mention that in the interview somehow. But my centerpieces will be front and center!" Mom clutches her hands and laughs. "Get it? Centerpiece. Front and center." She frowns at my lack of response but then wanders off to work on another table.

"Nice," I grumble. As I begin to sprinkle the gems, I notice Jasper staring at me. "What?"

"I get it. That's why you were arguing with Ashley. You two were supposed to match or something, right? Anne of Green Gables doesn't seem like you, because it's not."

"I said I didn't really want to talk about it anymore. You heard your mom, right? There's no way I'm going to be able to raise enough money to get Grampa back home. And my friendship with Ashley is over. You'll be happy to know you were right. Some things can't be fixed."

Jasper straightens. "I don't think you can fix things by sneaking around and not acting like yourself. And since you brought it up, you know who does seem happy? Your grampa." He takes his baggie and storms off.

I can't imagine how tonight could go any worse. Across the room, Mom straightens a tablecloth then pulls out her pocket tape measure, and I wish I could set up my life like Mom stages one of her tables—with everything working out just like I'd planned.

I'm tossing rhinestones when a woman with an orange blazer and a cat-ear headband sits down at the table I'm bedazzling. She nods to my baggie of gems. "Is your mom responsible for these tables? I'm guessing you must be related since you're helping out." She points to Mom's centerpiece. "They're amazing. We have a segment called 'Local Wonders,' and I'm thinking of doing a piece on your mom for our evening show. I'm Ginger Raines from KTEN news."

She reaches out her hand and I shake it. Maybe it's hearing her use the word *wonder*, but the more I think, the more an idea slowly opens like a blooming rose. Jasper might be right about the costume, but he's wrong about Grampa.

"You know she's got a shot at winning the National Expo competition tomorrow," I say.

"National, huh? I didn't even know there was such a thing as tablescaping until a few days ago," Ginger says.

"It's a big deal. This is the first year it's been held in Oklahoma, and there's some sort of contest to appear on a new show hosted by Arletta Paisley.

I'm sure she'd love to talk to you about it." I scatter another handful of rhinestones.

"Arletta Paisley?" Ginger asks. "You mean *Top Table?*" I nod, and she heads off in Mom's direction.

Mom is focused on the KTEN reporter, Grampa is nowhere to be seen, and Jasper is helping restock the refreshments and actively ignoring me. No one notices when I take Mom's empty rolling suitcase. Creepy music starts up, drowning out the rumble of the wheels across the linoleum.

Grampa's room is quiet and dark. I don't need the lights on to see Dr. Jon on his windowsill roost. If that tiny wooden horse was worth twenty-two thousand dollars, then Dr. Jon has to be worth twice as much. He's sure twice as big. I lay mom's suitcase flat on the floor, gently place Dr. Jon inside, and leave a quick note in his place.

Hope your feathers aren't too ruffled but don't suspect fowl play. I just felt cooped up and needed to stretch my wings.
    Hugs & Pecks,
    Dr. Jon

On the walk to the elevator my heart is hammering so hard I'm surprised it's not louder than the racket coming from the social room. Leaving the note doesn't make taking Dr. Jon right, but maybe Grampa won't worry too much. I can't risk his saying no if I'd asked first.

I make it downstairs and am greeted by the smiling woman working the front desk and operating the doors.

"Hi, I just need to get something from my mom's trunk." I motion to the rolling suitcase. "I'll be right back."

"Sure, hon," she says, opens the doors, and goes back to reading a magazine.

Mom never locks her car. I pop the trunk, take Dr. Jon out of the suitcase, and shove him under the extra Bubble Wrap she keeps there just in case.

I walk through the first set of doors, rolling Mom's empty suitcase behind me and am buzzed in. By the time I get to the social room again, it's even more crowded. I wind my way through all the other family members and residents, slide the suitcase back where I found it, and sidle right up to Mom.

She leans down. "Where've you been?"

"Bathroom," I whisper. "Where's Grampa?"

"Getting made up for the show, I guess." Mom laughs and points. "Speak of the devil." The hallway is teeming with residents, some zombie walking, some rolling in wheelchairs or using canes and walkers, but all wearing torn clothes and grayish-green face makeup. When I finally spot Grampa, it isn't his gruesome face paint that takes my breath away. He's walking! Seeing Grampa come shuffling in looking closer to his old self feels like whatever had a squeezing hold on my heart lets go for a second, and I take a good, deep breath for the first time since seeing those business cards in Mom's bag.

I almost run over to tell him how this is definitely a *step* in the right direction, but I freeze when I see those gold-striped Adidas sneakers. Toni hooks her arm through his and he gives his new lopsided smile to her.

Grampa would never move on without me. Would he?

The audience starts laughing and clapping. And I do too, but each time my hands meet I'm less sure that I've done the right thing. Especially when I see Jasper smiling and standing next to his mom.

The residents come to the front of the room, some sit in chairs, some stand. They relax their necks and drop their heads. As the music begins, they start moving their shoulders to the beat. There's a howling wolf in the background, and when the singing starts, they lift their heads quickly and hiss.

Mr. Curtis's family is screaming with laughter— partly because he's brushed his hair so it's standing on end, but he's also taken his front teeth out. All the performers place their hands on their knees and sort of walk them up their legs until the lyrics say something about stopping hearts, then they grab their chest. They swing their arms from side to side with the music and make horrible faces while trying not to crack up. Even grouchy Mrs. Wingfield is laughing.

When Michael Jackson sings about screaming, they all whip their head toward the audience and actually scream—a few people in the crowd do too. As the song ends, Grampa and his new friends hold their hands up in claws and bare their teeth like vampires.

The whole room goes wild, clapping and whistling, and the residents bow as they get a standing ovation. I don't know if I've ever seen Grampa have so much fun. He's laughing and smiling more than when we found that wheat penny worth almost two thousand dollars stuck to the bottom of an old tennis shoe.

We spend the rest of the evening meeting the families of Grampa's friends, including Toni's son and grandchildren. Even though I know Grampa must want to go home, he sure isn't acting like it.

There are so many introductions, I don't get a moment alone with Grampa. Before we leave, Mom does something I've never seen her do before—she gives Grampa a kiss on the cheek. Even though I'm a little mad at both of them, I walk over to his side and give him a small squeeze.

Taking Dr. Jon is wrong, but what I have planned could change everything back to the way it was, back to normal, in one fell swoop, or in this case, one fowl swoop. So, I keep my mouth shut and make it through the rest of the night without telling him that

I borrowed his most prized possession. I also give him three more hugs.

There's no way to avoid Jasper as we leave. Mom chats with his mom while he and I shuffle around and avoid eye contact. Amanda waves as we get into the elevator.

"Thanks again for giving Mabel a lift." Mom nudges me.

"Yeah, thank you," I say. "Bye, Jasper."

The doors close before he has a chance to say anything back.

When we get home, I help Mom unload the car, careful to get everything she used for her centerpieces from the trunk so she won't poke around there. Once I bring in the last load, Mom stretches and then wraps me in a hug. "Thanks for all your help tonight. I couldn't do any of this without you. I think I'll take a quick shower." She gives me a kiss on the cheek and walks down the hall. She's forgotten all about the dance and my problems, and any chance I might tell her a single thing evaporates.

As soon as I hear the water turn on, I quietly sneak out, get Dr. Jon, and lug him up the stairs and into my room. My heart is slamming against my ribs, and my bangs are sweat-stuck to my forehead as I wrap Dr. Jon in a towel from my hamper and tuck him under my bed. He barely fits.

My gramma thought Dr. Jon was magical, and even though I know it's silly, I sure hope she was right.

23

MOM KNOCKS ON MY DOOR. I BOLT UPRIGHT AND close my computer. My plan required a bit of private research.

She squeezes water from her hair with a towel, a towel that matches the one wrapped around Dr. Jon. "Hey, do you feel like talking about whatever happened at the Fall Festival now?" She nods toward the kitchen. "Come on. I'll make us some hot cocoa."

Grampa and I have a few secrets we keep from Mom but nothing big, nothing like what I've been up to lately. But I could say the same for her. Sitting there on the edge of my bed with Dr. Jon just out of view and Mom standing in my doorway, it feels like I have a swarming hill of fire ants inside me, and I don't like the feeling one bit.

Once we're at the dining table blowing the surface of steaming mugs, Mom looks over at me. "I feel like you've got a lot going on lately that you're not telling me."

"I think there's a lot you're not telling me too." I cross my arms and lean back from the table, for once clear of any of Mom's decorations. Everything's packed in her other rolling suitcases or rolled up in Bubble Wrap and carefully tucked into boxes.

Mom sighs. "All right, I know you have questions, but let me tell you some things first." She folds her hands together and takes a deep breath. "Grampa offered to let me sell some of Gramma's things. He's left everything she owned sitting right where it was the day she died. Sometimes holding on to something isn't healthy."

Mom won't meet my eye. "I've been saving for years. Grampa and I talked about it before all this happened. He won't let me use the money to pay for Whispering Pines. It's to buy half the business. Once Patty and I are equal partners, I'll make more. Maybe enough to cover Grampa's care. If and when he comes home, he'll still need speech and physical therapy, probably occupational therapy too." Mom trails off and is quiet for a second. "Either way, the extra money I'll bring in from Pattie's will solve a lot of our worries. I have to think long term."

"What about Grampa's house?" I ask.

Mom's eyebrows shoot up. "Grampa told you?"

I answer with a shrug.

"He's got to make a decision soon. Because Grampa's house is in Lakehaven, it's worth a lot of money. Selling it would give him more options. Things will have to change, honey. Fighting it only makes it harder. On you and everyone else."

Time to test the water. "But what if we could see what Dr. Jon is worth? Maybe then you wouldn't have to sell any of Grampa's other stuff."

Saying Dr. Jon out loud helps me work up the nerve to tell her my plan. But before I get the chance,

Mom scoffs. "If that thing is worth the twenty dollars your gramma paid for it, I'd be shocked. Besides, I'm not selling any of Grampa's stuff. I'm selling Gramma's wedding china, her silverware, and her old vanity desk. Lord knows, I don't have any room for it in this tiny apartment." Mom gives me a sad smile. "Sometimes you have to let grown-ups handle the hard decisions."

I should've known she wouldn't listen to me. At least she's not selling Grampa's collections, but still. I can't imagine not having Grampa's house in my life. Normally I keep the bad maybes to myself, but a few push their way right out of my mouth before I can stop them. "Maybe Pattie won't ever make you a partner. Maybe she's just using you like she always does."

Mom straightens and narrows her eyes. "What do you mean? She's told me for years that once I had the money, she'd draw up the paperwork. She's seventy years old, for goodness' sake."

I can't stop myself. "Exactly. She's made you lots of promises that never happened."

Mom stands up. "I know you must've had a difficult evening, but you know how hard I've worked for this and how important tomorrow is to me."

"Did you ever think that maybe I don't care about tomorrow. Maybe I have my own problems going on. Maybe I don't even want to go at all!" I bang the table without meaning to.

The look on Mom's face is one I haven't seen before. There's no hint of softness in her voice when she says, "Don't go, then. I'll call Jerry in the morning and see if you can spend the day with them."

Mom walks back to her room. The door slamming doesn't hurt as much as knowing that going with Mom is more appealing than going to Ashley's house.

I look at Mom's largest rolling suitcase. There's only one thing left to do. I tiptoe to my room. Dr. Jon's wooden chest feels cool even through the layer of terry cloth.

My backpack holds everything I'll need for tomorrow's overnight stay at the Expo. The little spider pin glints up at me and I whisper, "It's now or never." There's no way I can squeeze Dr. Jon in there along with everything else. So, I carry him to the table and unclick the latches of Mom's giant red suitcase as quietly as I can. Once I take out extra Bubble Wrap and the mini hay bales Mom is using to protect her precious boot centerpiece, he fits perfectly.

24

WE WAKE UP BEFORE THE SUN AND LOAD OUR car with Mom's supplies. The only words she says to me are orders. "Be careful." "Don't jostle that around." "That's a box of dishes, not a snow globe." I make sure I'm the one who carries the red suitcase. She's bound to notice the difference in weight, and then it's all over for me and my plan.

Neither of us bring up the argument. I'm still mad, and her bossing me around, plus the orange sweater, only adds to it.

When I roll the suitcase to the trunk she says, "Let me help you with that."

"I've got it," I say. But as I try to hide how hard it is to lift and gently lower into the trunk, I feel so unsure it must show on my face.

"What's wrong with you?" she asks. But what she really means is whatever's wrong with me I better just get over it, because she has bigger things to worry about today. So, I say nothing, climb in the back with the boxes instead of the front, and fasten my seat buckle.

"Sure, I don't mind being the chauffeur, your highness," Mom grumbles as she gets in, slams her door, and starts the car.

The drive takes even longer because we get stuck behind a tractor for part of the way. I fall asleep and only wake up when Mom says, "We're here." She turns and gives me a smile. Either the time driving or her nerves about the competition have softened her mood toward me. I can't say the same.

I empty the contents of my backpack in the back seat of the car. Maybe I can figure out a way to get Dr. Jon from mom's case and into my bag, then sneak over to the appraisal. Mom looks at what I've done and raises an eyebrow.

"Thought I'd take my empty bag in case we find something we want to buy, then I can carry it in here," I say.

"Well, I don't know that we'll have time to shop." She pins a flyaway curl back into her bun. "We better head over and start setting up."

"Okay." I throw my bag over my shoulder. We unpack the trunk and I grab the red suitcase by the handle.

"Careful with that one. It's got the centerpiece. Something goes wrong with that and I might as well go home now."

The Tulsa convention center is a whole lot bigger than the venues we've been to before. There are the normal booths of crafts, but there are also food trucks, an indoor farmers market, and even a full-size carousel. Huge banners hang from the metal rafters advertising *Collector's Menagerie* and the new show *Top Table*. Mom smiles when she sees the shock on my face.

"It's like they moved a whole state fair inside, isn't it?" she asks.

I only nod and move out of the way of a couple

of Mandalorians, followed by a rolling cart topped with two cats in Victorian gowns pushed by a woman dressed to match.

"Whoa," I say. "I hope those guys aren't on one of the tables."

Mom laughs. "There's some sort of cat show and costume competition in here too. Being so close to Halloween, I imagine we'll see quite a few costumes today."

We approach a wide-open entrance with turnstiles and doormen all wearing dark blue shirts and hats with a familiar golden logo. There's a banner bearing a tagline I instantly recognize:

COLLECTOR'S MENAGERIE: SHARE YOUR TREASURES WITH THE WORLD.

Mom puts a hand on my shoulder. "When we're done setting up maybe we'll have time to poke around."

I swallow hard and manage to nod.

Mom checks her paperwork. "We need to find table thirteen. Yikes, thirteen."

"Well, it is the day before Halloween. So, maybe thirteen is lucky today."

Mom gives me a doubtful look as I catch a glimpse of a sign for tablescaping and a familiar roped-off area full of empty tables. I point just as Wonder Woman and Captain Marvel walk by. "Let's take that as a good sign," I say.

Mom laughs. "I sure hope you're right."

We find table 13 and wheel over our suitcases. Mom scans her table and even leans over to eyeball it up close, making sure it's level. She brushes her hand across the top, and after a deep breath, says, "Well, let's get to it."

I stand there trying to think up some reason to get her away from the table long enough for me to get Dr. Jon into my backpack. Then I could just say I need to go to the bathroom, rush over to the Main Hall, get Dr. Jon appraised, and be back before she even knows I'm gone. It's not a great plan, but it's all I've got.

Or I could tell her. Maybe she'd even come with me?

I reach for the dinner plates.

"Careful, those are handmade to look like worn stoneware. I want to hold off on putting them out until I get the hay down." At the mention of hay, my heart stops.

She pulls out a big bag of hay, the kind they sell for guinea pigs and rabbits at the pet store. For a moment, I'm relieved, but then she says, "I also have seven tiny hay bales that form a little pyramid under the centerpiece. They make it just the right height. It's going to be sheer perfection." Mom squeezes her hands under her chin. "The boots weren't going to work, and then I found those miniature bales in the Halloween department at the hardware store. It was fate. Those little hay bales solved all my problems."

I'm frozen, standing there holding one of her handmade plates. She's talking about the hay around the boots, the hay that I took out so Dr. Jon would fit in the suitcase, the hay that is right now sitting under our dining room table over an hour away. "Those weren't just packing so the boots wouldn't shift around?" I ask.

Mom is focused on sprinkling hay. "Oh no, those

saved my centerpiece. I thought I was going to have to start from scratch. No, this time I didn't have to use nearly as much Bubble Wrap, with all this hay." Mom laughs.

The next few minutes pass like I'm underwater, like I just need to break the surface, take a deep breath, and tell Mom what I've done. What *have* I done? Because I wanted to get money, to sell Grampa's heart find, I've cost Mom a win she's been working toward for years.

Mom starts to unwrap her showstopper. I take a deep breath. "Mom, I have something to tell you."

She holds a hand up. "Wait, me first. I made this as a surprise for you."

She pulls away the last piece of packing paper. It's an antique window complete with peeling paint and a country scene affixed to the back of the panes so that when it sits on the edge of the table there's a view looking out into a field. It's sort of brilliant, but also familiar.

"What do you think?" she asks. "I borrowed it from Grampa's backyard. I thought it might be nice to have a little bit of his energy here for good luck. Plus, it's what you've always suggested, working in pieces with some character and heart. I think I finally understand why it's special for you two."

"I love it," I say, and for once, I mean it. "It's perfect."

Mom smiles. "Maybe even better than perfect?"

I nod and my eyes fill with tears. Mom steps toward me and hands over a paper towel. "Oh now, don't overreact."

"Mom—" She interrupts me again and dangles something in my face that looks like the snaps from a pair of short suspenders.

"These are the napkin holders! I ordered a pair of toddler overalls and cut the straps off. A genius move, if I do say so myself."

Speaking of genius moves, I accidentally left part of your decorations so that I could bring along something I stole from Grampa, hoping we can take the money and bring Grampa back home. Nope, that's not going to work.

Mom, I was wrong. Your tables are *like a collection. And I'm sorry I didn't see it before now. Before I ruined everything.* That's a start.

I open my mouth just as Mom reaches for the red suitcase.

"Mom, wait," I say.

She looks up at me, still smiling over her napkin holders when her eyes narrow a little. "How did you know I had hay packed around my centerpiece?"

We both see a flash of sequins at the same time. Lorna Diamond, dressed in her signature glitz, makes her way through the tables, catching light like a walking disco ball, and heads straight for us.

Lorna walks right up to Mom and says, "I want to apologize for my behavior at our last competition. You created a divine table that deserved the win. I acted like a spoiled child, and I'm sorry."

Mom is so shocked she's not even bothering to hide it. She opens and closes her mouth a few times before she's able to reply. "Well, thank you for that, Lorna."

Lorna nods as I hear Mom unlatch the suitcase and open it.

"Wait," I manage to get out before Mom gasps. Lorna peeks around the open suitcase and gasps too.

25

LORNA LEANS IN FOR A CLOSER LOOK. "OH, I'VE thought about bringing an alternate and deciding in the moment, but I've never had the guts to do it." Lorna shakes her head. "Jane, you're more daring than I thought. I better go set up. Good luck!"

"To you too, Lorna." Mom forces a smile.

The whole time they talk, I feel this heaviness, like the cry-knot I've carried around lately is about to sink me through the floor.

As soon as Lorna is out of earshot, Mom whips around and hisses, "You better explain yourself right this instant." I take a deep breath and get ready to spill everything, but before I have the chance Mom goes on. "Where are the rest of the hay bales? Does your grampa know you took his statue? What in the world are you trying to pull?"

"Mom, I took the hay out. I thought it was there to keep the boots from rolling around. I was going take Dr. Jon over to be appraised. Just to see what he's worth. With the money we could keep Grampa's house or pay for him to have a nurse or therapist or whatever."

"Dr. Jon." Mom scoffs, shakes her head, and puts her hands over her face. She looks up and says, "Mabel, I don't even know what to say to you right now."

Finally, I let go of the thing that's weighed on me the most. "I lied to Grampa that morning, and I didn't go meet him because I was embarrassed about our hunts, and he had a stroke and was alone all because of me." I look right at Mom until I get every last word out.

She sighs and comes to stand by me. "Grampa's stroke was absolutely not your fault."

"Maybe not." I nod toward her table. "But this is."

Mom's mouth is pinched in an unforgiving line. "I can't believe you would do this. Without talking to me, without asking Grampa? You know how important today is for me. How seriously I take my tables. And you know how important that"—Mom motions to Dr. Jon— "thing is to him."

"Oh, I know." Without meaning to, a little sarcasm sneaks into my words. "You're always so focused on this stuff and everything being *perfect.*"

Mom sighs and looks at her table. "Well, it certainly isn't perfect now." She turns back to me. "I'm focused on my tables because winning makes me feel valued, like I'm really good at something. Perfection is what wins here." Mom shakes her head. "I'll get over it." Then she lifts the boots she worked on for a month. "With time." She starts arranging the sprigs of wheat and fake daisies. "Are you going to stand there or help?"

I wipe my cheeks and pull out the candles wrapped in wax paper. Mom already lit them at home and let them burn, tilting them so that the wax dripped down the side exactly the way she wanted. She's even snipped off the singed part off the wick, so they looked new and old at the same time.

We step back from her table. She sighs again, pulls out her measuring tape, and uses it on the tallest candle and the centerpiece. "With the four inches gone they're exactly the same height. Varying height is central to a cohesive table. It's a Principles and Elements deduction for sure. And if I take the candle away and have only the two, it'll look unbalanced. Another deduction." She lifts her hands, palms up. "I don't know what to do. And with Arletta Paisley here as a guest judge..."

"I'm sorry," I say.

Mom nods. "I know you are." She gives me a sad smile. "Well, it is what it is. Let's take some of this stuff back to the car. Then I think I'm going to need a milkshake."

We don't talk as we load up the car and make our way back to the convention center. I'm carrying Dr. Jon in my backpack. He doesn't quite fit, and I can't zip my bag all the way. Mom sure doesn't offer to help or to let me roll him around in one of her suitcases again. Once inside, we manage to find milkshakes and an empty table in the food court.

Mom checks her phone over and over, anxious

about the judging. It's about half an hour before we can enter the Main Hall and I'll finally see what Dr. Jon is worth. But I'm not excited. In fact, every time I think about it, I feel like crying. Mom's lost the competition before it's even started. Because of me and four inches.

My backpack sits stiff and round beside my chair with the points of Dr. Jon's wings pulling the fabric taut and his head sticking out from the top. The spider pin flashes green, and I think of my last hunt with Grampa. I think of heart finds, and how they're like a bridge from one person's heart to another, and how the only heart I've been thinking about lately is my own. And suddenly I know what to do. "Mom, about how tall would you say your centerpiece was with the hay bales?"

Mom shrugs, then says, "About exactly two feet."

I crouch, unzip my bag, and heave Dr. Jon to the middle of our table. Mom slowly leans around to look at me, her eyes wide.

"What says farm more than a rooster? That's why Lorna thought you'd brought an alternate. She thought Dr. Jon was one of your options. He's perfect." After what I've done lately, the lying and sneaking around and thinking the worst of her, maybe Dr. Jon might save me after all.

"But don't you have to line up for the appraisal?" Mom asks.

"What about we pull a double switcheroo? Remember that time part of Tamela Carter's centerpiece was stolen once the judging was over? They ruled it wasn't grounds for disqualification because the official rules state that the table can't be altered after the bell for setup and the judging starts. The rules don't say anything about after the judging is complete. Once the judging ends the scores are final, right?"

"Poor Tamela has the worst luck." Mom nods. "I don't think I have much to lose at this point. Let's go."

We toss our milkshakes and make a run for it, more like an awkward jog with Dr. Jon in tow and Mom in heels.

As we get to Mom's table, I see a group of men and women with clipboards gathering. "I think the judges are here." One judge stands out from the rest; she has carefully curled blond hair, a little too much makeup on, and a tight denim blazer. "Is that Arletta?"

Mom nods and checks her phone. "I've got fifteen minutes until the bell."

She rips the fake wheat from the old centerpiece and shoves the empty boots over to me. The stems of the stalks are actually wire so they can be bent. She arranges them in a thick sunburst shape under Dr. Jon's base and bends each one slightly upward. Then she takes the daisies, snips their stems off, and sticks them here and there in the wheat. When she steps back, the overall height difference is perfect, and it looks like Dr. Jon has roosted in a nest made by country fairies.

I watch in awe. Grampa always says I have a feel for picking, but it seems to me Mom's got a feel for this. The way she reimagined her centerpiece all inside a few minutes beats any restoration project Grampa and I ever did. Mom's got a gift, and she deserves this win and to be a contestant on *Top Table*. She smiles and even gives me a wink as an alarm sounds and the judges gather around the first table.

The Expo works a little differently than the other competitions Mom's done. They do the judging today, open the tables to the public, and announce scores the following morning rather than post them.

Mom and I stand outside the corded-off area with all the other tablescapers and a slowly gathering crowd of Expo attendees.

"When do you have to line up for the appraisal?" Mom asks.

Thirty minutes ago. "Soon," I say, and try to smile so Mom doesn't sense my lie. At least this fib might actually fix something. Mom hugs her old leather-boot centerpiece tight with one arm, smiles back, and surprises me by reaching down and holding my hand. As the judges near Mom's table, she squeezes.

The scoring takes forever, and by the time they've finished the last table and opened the area to the public again, I'm over an hour late. Mom and I approach her table with the other spectators. "I'll just slip under the ropes and switch him out for the boots." Mom crosses her fingers. "Here's to hoping no one notices."

"Mom, don't. Since this competition is different than the others and the final scores aren't announced until tomorrow, maybe the rules are different. I don't think we can risk it."

"But I thought the plan was I'd swap him out, and

you run over for the appraisal, and we put him right back?" Mom asks.

"I might've bent the truth a little. The appraisals were almost two hours ago." I shrug. "This is something you deserve. You've earned a chance to win." I nod toward Mom's new centerpiece. "Whenever Grampa and I find something special, we try to imagine what its next purpose could be. I think this is Dr. Jon's next purpose. Besides, heart finds are supposed to connect people, and now he connects all of us—Gramma, me, Grampa, and after today, you too."

"I know another thing your grampa says." Mom looks at me. "Sometimes you don't find what you expected, but just what your heart needed." She squeezes my hand again and stares at me the same way Grampa did when we found my Amberina basket.

26

THAT EVENING WE WATCH TWO OLD MOVIES THAT
Mom loves, *The Wedding Planner* and *The Wedding Singer*.
We lay across from each other in our identical full-size
beds. I can't think of the last time Mom and I slept in
the same room.

When the second movie ends, Mom reaches over
and turns off the lamp on the nightstand. The thick
curtains, the hum of the AC unit, the weight of the
blankets—it's all different from home. Even though I
know I did the right thing for once, and maybe even
fixed something I messed up, I still feel so far away

from what's familiar. A few tears slide down my face and soak into the pillow.

"You okay?" Mom asks.

"I have to tell you one more thing." I figure I better go on and tell the whole truth. "I've been going on hunts with Jasper, trying to raise money for Grampa's house. I made a little under three hundred dollars."

"Mabel, I can't have you scavenging without a grown-up. It isn't safe. Something you need to keep in mind is that this is Grampa's decision. I wasn't the one who came up with the idea of selling the house, he was."

"What?"

"Of course. You don't think I'd sell his house without his input, do you?"

I sort of did, but I'm not about to admit it. "I just can't imagine him anywhere else."

"Well, you know your grampa. Just takes one look at his yard to know he's good at reimagining things. He says he's ready to let go. I think that house holds a lot of memories that've kept your grampa from moving on." I sniff again and Mom clears her throat. "I have a confession to make too. I've always been a little envious of the relationship you have with Grampa."

"Really?" I sit up, but it's so dark all I see is her shadowy outline.

"You two are so close. I've never been like that with him. Not even when I was your age. My mom was his special someone. I was sort of a lonely kid." Mom is quiet before she says what I'm thinking. "We were so close when you were little, but not so much anymore. I think that's why I pushed you to do these competitions, trying to force you to spend time with me. You know these pearls I wear were a gift from Grampa on the day you were born. He gave them to me at the hospital. They remind me of what I realized the first time I held you, that if I did my best, maybe I'd never have to be lonely again."

"Mom…" I start.

"I'm not finished," she says. "Today didn't go the way either of us wanted. But I had fun with you."

"Me too," I say.

"You have some very innovative tablescaping ideas, and I think we should do more things together. If you want," Mom adds. "And I love you."

I laugh. "I love you too, Mom."

"One last thing I should've said a long time ago." Mom's bed creaks as she sits up too. "Some changes we can control and some we can't. But you and I have each other, and no matter what happens, it'll be okay. Change can sometimes leave a space for something new to grow."

A few more tears sneak their way down my cheeks. I nod, though I know she can't see me. Maybe me and Mom and Grampa can figure out what new thing we want to grow, together this time.

.～✺～.

Mom and I wake up to the sound of an unfamiliar phone ringing—our wake-up call from the front desk. Mom answers, mumbles a thank-you, then grabs her cell phone. "Goodness," she says. "I have a few messages from Amanda, Jasper's mom."

I sit up too, worried something is wrong with Grampa. But then Mom starts scrolling through and smiling. "Oh, that's sweet," she says, and I relax. "She's found a channel broadcasting the judging results, and they're going to watch from Whispering

Pines." Mom yawns. "What do you think? Shower or just go down and eat some continental breakfast?"

I stretch. "Just head down."

"Well, I'm going to shower." She gets up and takes her outfit into the bathroom.

I sit on the end of the bed, thinking about how badly I treated Jasper and how much I have to tell Grampa. There's a whole pile of things I still need to fix.

.⁓ℓℓ⁓.

Once we dress, we eat breakfast and then make our way over to the convention center. Mom and I explore the booths, and Mom even buys me a basket she finds at a hand-blown glass table. At eleven thirty she says, "Well, should we head over?"

I nod and we walk toward the area outside the Main Hall. The navy banner is still there. Mom looks over at me and says, "Remember, whatever happens, it'll be okay." Mom hooks her arm through mine, and I hope that she's right.

Next to the tablescaping area, a small stage has been erected overnight. The empty mic stand sets my nerves on edge right away. Mom's phone buzzes from inside her purse. When she looks at the screen, she mumbles, "Amanda wants to know where we are so Grampa can keep an eye out for us."

Just then I see something that makes me laugh out loud. "I don't think they're actually watching us on TV."

"What makes you say that?" Mom asks, her attention still on her phone. I touch her forearm and point. Jasper and his mom are slowly making their way through the food court. And they're not alone. Amanda is pushing Grampa in a wheelchair.

Mom covers her mouth in shock. I'm only happy for a moment before I realize Grampa is going to see Dr. Jon sitting on the table. And there's Jasper and his big smile. I've had so many heart-to-hearts with Mom in the past twenty-four hours that my heart is sort of worn out, but if I want to make things right, I have more work to do.

We meet halfway, and Grampa says, "Surprise." He holds his left arm out to hug Mom.

"Technically, your grampa isn't cleared for a day pass until Monday, but I pulled some strings,"

Amanda says. Mom and I both hug Amanda, and then we hug Grampa again. I bump Jasper with my forearm.

"I think I had a hard time figuring out what to let go of and what to hold on to. You were right, and I didn't want to admit—" He holds up his hand and gives me a hug.

A small screech from the sound system comes from the stage, and we all make our way over. The tables are still set from the day before, but scores aren't posted.

As we walk, I lean down to Grampa and say, "I'm sorry and I should've asked first."

Grampa looks confused. I motion to Mom's table. When he sees Dr. Jon he gasps and says, "Looks like he landed just where he needed to be." I grab his hand, he squeezes mine, and I hope that means I'm forgiven.

27

WE STROLL AROUND LOOKING AT ALL THE OTHER tables, including one with an enormous American flag sprouting from Uncle Sam's top hat along with red, white, and royal blue silk roses. Grampa looks at me, nods toward the table, and says, "It's a little over the top—over the top hat, that is." Then he tries to waggle his eyebrows. Mom and I look at each other and roll our eyes at the same time. Grampa, Amanda, and Jasper laugh.

A man in a brown suit takes the stage and taps the mic. Mom's eyes widen and she leans down to whisper, "That's Bud Ludlow, king of the showstopper."

I try my best to look impressed. Mom wears the tightest of smiles and manages a few claps for each announcement.

Bud clears his throat and takes a long pause. "For this year's Best in Show winner we have a very special prize. It's my honor to introduce our guest judge, Arletta Paisley." The same woman I spotted yesterday takes the stage. Her hair hasn't moved an inch, but this time she wears a heavily embroidered shirt and skinny jeans with boots. The crowd is clapping and whistling and taking photos. Mom gives me a wide-eyed look that cracks me up.

Arletta waves and smiles before speaking. "I've been blown away by some of the dining environments I've seen this weekend. There's nothing quite like sitting down for dinner at a table that's been set by a visionary, and I think every single one of the designers here are true artists. But there was one table that took my breath away. Lorna Diamond, I was truly inspired by your interpretation of our theme, and it's my pleasure to give you the first-place ribbon for the Expert Division, the Best in Show trophy, and a spot as one of the first contestants on my new show, *Top Table*."

Mom's shoulders droop, but she claps just as hard as anyone else.

Once the applause dies down, Arletta goes on. "We have a few more announcements to make. Bud tells me this award was introduced last year. The Crowd Pleaser goes to the table with the most votes from the Expo attendees. Jane Cunningham, who I hear is a new up-and-comer, took the theme and created a truly inspired table. She may be our second-place winner, but she came in first with the crowd. Table thirteen achieved something special—a look that is both old and new, and purposeful while still being spontaneous. Jane, you'll be taking home a ribbon and a trophy too, and I truly hope you'll consider applying for *Top Table* next season."

Jasper blows a loud whistle with his fingers in his mouth, and his mom blushes while Mom and I hug and hop around a bit. Grampa stands from his wheelchair and wraps up Mom in a big hug too. And we all huddle together and clap for Mom when she takes the stage, shakes hands with Bud and Arletta, and accepts her trophy and red ribbon.

After all the announcements, Mom poses for a few photos, one standing beside her table with all the judges. Then it's up to us to pack up, but with all of us working together it takes no time at all.

As we approach the double set of automatic doors, Grampa activates the brakes. Mom stumbles into the back of his wheelchair. He's staring into the lobby and raises a shaky finger to point at a man with a poof of blond bangs and a wide, bright smile.

Ray Reno, *Collector's Menagerie*'s appraising superstar, is in the lobby.

Grampa looks up at me and lifts Dr. Jon a little. "What do you say, Mae-mae, should we go ask him?"

I nod, unable to speak. Grampa hands Dr. Jon to me and uses the armrests to push himself up. Grampa and I haven't held hands since I was little, but I hitch Dr. Jon up on my hip so that we can now.

Ray seems to know immediately why we're there. He smiles and stretches his hand out toward Grampa. "Ray Reno. You two fans of the show?"

I nod, and Grampa says, "We watch every Monday evening together."

Ray smiles and nods toward Dr. Jon. "Want me to take a look?"

"We'd be honored," Grampa says, and gently nudges me. I hold Dr. Jon out. Ray takes him, and motions to a few chairs lining the windows of the convention center. "Let's have a seat."

I can't believe I'm sitting by Ray Reno.

"What do we have here?" Ray mumbles as he turns Dr. Jon this way and that.

Grampa doesn't say anything, so I do. "He's my Grampa's. He's a wooden rooster. Not a chicken. And he was discovered in Florida in a shop called Second Chances about twelve years ago. That's all I know. And he's special." For once, Mom doesn't scoff, but I realize without the historical whimsy, the actual facts of Dr. Jon aren't nearly as impressive.

Ray starts talking, and at first, I'm only watching his mouth move instead of listening. When I tune in, he says, "Many folk artists favored farm animals, and quite a few famous sculptors came out of Pennsylvania. I'd say Wilhelm Schimmel is one of the most famous of America's folk carvers. And this definitely has echoes of his style." Ray lifts Dr. Jon and inspects the base. I know already there are no markings. "Schimmel's work is hard to identify because it's well known that he didn't leave any type of signature. We mostly have to rely on family stories and formal verification."

Grampa pats my hand. As soon as Ray said the word *echo* I knew, and Grampa must too. An echo means to repeat or imitate the original. It's a nice way to call Dr. Jon a fake. And even though I feel like I might cave in and cry again right there, I prepare for the details because I know that's what is coming next.

When Ray looks at me his brow furrows. I take a deep breath before he says, "It's a very inspired imitation of Schimmel's style and extremely popular with collectors. I'd say he'd fetch two to three hundred dollars at auction." Ray pats Dr. Jon's head and he flashes his brilliantly white teeth. "And I do agree with you. He's special."

Mom steps forward and rests a hand on my shoulder. "Thank you," she says to Ray. Grampa finally talks. "Ray, it's been a pleasure." He stands and shakes Ray's hand again. I lean my head on Mom's shoulder and try my hardest not to cry in front of Ray Reno.

We turn to walk off and Ray says, "Hold on a sec there." He stands and points to my backpack. "That spider pin on your bag, would you mind if I have a closer look at that?"

"Sure," I say. The latch is tricky, so it takes me a minute to unhook the pin. I place the little spider on Ray's palm. He holds it close and turns it over, then he whistles. "I'm not a jewelry expert, but I'd get this beauty appraised." He points to the green stone. "That little fleck of black there is an impurity, and that flaw in the stone normally indicates you've got a real gem, not a fake. I think it's a genuine emerald. The setting is very Edwardian. Maybe even platinum. And the detailing, the onyx eyes and the little pearls along the legs... Extraordinary." He passes my pin back. "I can't tell you what it's worth exactly, but I might not carry it around on my backpack if I were you." Ray laughs and shakes hands with Grampa again before walking outside.

Grampa looks over at me and smiles. "Another day full of treasures," he says, the same way he would anytime we wrapped up a hunt. We walk out together. Mom helps Grampa into Jasper's minivan. I climb in and hug him around the neck. "I'm sorry I took your heart find."

He pats my back and says, "Don't be silly. You and your mom, those are the only heart finds I need. Love you, Mae-mae."

"Love you too, Grampa." I hug his neck again and Mom surprises us both when she clambers in and wraps her arms around the two of us. I whisper, "I think Gramma was right about Dr. Jon." I feel Grampa laugh and Mom nodding.

Mom thanks Amanda again. I turn to Jasper. "Was this your idea?"

He shrugs and smiles.

"Thank you," I say.

"No problem. I'll see you in a few hours to trick-or-treat with McKenna, right?"

I nod.

This time I stay awake for the drive home. Mom explains that Grampa thinks selling his house is the best option. "So, over the next few months I'll need your help to pack up his collections and take what he wants to keep and move it to the storage unit you two think I don't know about." Mom looks over at me and smiles. "But I'd also like you to help me pick out a few things for his room at Whispering Pines. I thought you'd like that idea."

"I do," I say.

We get home, and Mom grabs her trophy and ribbon. "Go ahead and leave the rest. I'll unpack it later. I know you want to go meet your friends to trick-or-treat."

Jasper didn't really let me apologize properly. So, I text him a picture I found of a woman in a formal ball gown wearing a beauty queen sash that says "apology." This is my formal apology for being a jerk.

I run to my room ready to wear the costume I'd planned. Mom gave me clear fishing twine to attach a few more plush cats and dogs to an umbrella, and I already have a raincoat and boots. My phone buzzes as I work. I pick it up and see that it's Jasper. Meet in an hour. Need me to bring your apron and hat? You left them in the van.

I remember how easily I let Ashley talk me out of what I wanted, and I get an idea. I run into the living room. "Mom, can you help me? I only have an hour. I need some pink paint, elastic, a magnifying glass, and your trench coat." The good thing about Mom's tablescaping is she has almost any supply I can dream up.

Mom nods, comes back with all I'd asked for, and we get to work. After about forty-five minutes we're done. Mom helps me position the elastic around my face so that the nose we made from a painted cardboard toilet paper tube covers my real one. She shakes her head. "Well, you do look awful cute."

"I need one more thing." I take off toward my room but pause in the hallway. "Thanks, Mom."

She laughs and says, "Anytime."

The little butterfly pin that I fished out for Ashley sits in my Amberina basket. I grab it and a piece of paper, and write, "Some things change and that's okay."

I hug Mom on my way out. The walk to Ashley's house feels a little strange, and by the time I'm on her porch knocking at the door my heart is pounding. She answers dressed in the RockStarz costume.

"I wanted to tell you I'm sorry that I yelled at you and called you a coward." I hand her the pin. As she reads the card, she bites her bottom lip and I think she might cry. But she doesn't.

"I'm sorry too. But you were right, I should've found a way to talk to you about it." She looks me up and down and laughs. "I really like your costume."

"Thanks." I nod and we just stand there for a bit looking at each other. "Okay, then." I take a deep breath and say, "Bye, Ashley."

"Bye, Mabel." Ashley waves and I head toward the bus stop.

McKenna is the first person I see when I round Magnolia Drive. She's wearing a poster board with a small 6 in one corner and a huge C in the middle. Under the C are the numbers 12.011. She runs toward me as soon as she sees me and holds her arms out "I'd hug you, but my costume won't cooperate. I'm Carbon," McKenna says. "The element. It's the basis of all life. And, added bonus, no hair spray.

What are you?" Jasper walks up behind her and gives me a quick hug. He's dressed as Percy Jackson again.

"Guess," I say, and hold up the magnifying glass.

McKenna shrugs but Jasper gives me a huge smile. "She's herself—a cunning ham."

"Bingo," I say. He reaches out and straightens the cardboard snout Mom helped me make. As we take off together, I realize I might not have saved Grampa's house, but I did find a few treasures of my own.

28

THE NEXT WEEKEND MOM WAKES ME BEFORE SUN-rise. We usually sleep in on the weekends, but that isn't the strange part. Her hair is covered with a bandanna, and she's wearing a pair of Grampa's gray coveralls.

I sit up and rub my eyes. "Mom, Halloween was last weekend."

"Very funny," she says. "These things are actually really comfortable." She does a little spin, stretches her leg out, and gently kicks my mattress. "Come on. We've got a lot to do."

Mom and I cooked up a plan to surprise Grampa

and have been working out the details all week. We pull into the driveway of his house just as the sun lights the sky in pinks and oranges. She kills the engine and asks, "Are you ready?"

I sigh and nod. I haven't been inside Grampa's house since he was hospitalized. Mom and I spend about an hour loading the car with some of Grampa's favorites, including his records, the record player, and his marble collection. As we carry out the final load, I look back at the hallway still lined with shelves. Since Grampa's not here, it doesn't really feel the same, but I think I'll ask him if I can keep his miscellaneous shelf. I walk out trying to remember what Grampa's heart needs most, and that it isn't this place anymore.

Mom and I head to the backyard just as Amanda drops off Jasper with a box of donuts. Then we really get to work.

We take the six wooden pallets that Grampa and I salvaged from SiteOne Landscape Supply back in the summer. Jasper removes every other wooden slat, and Mom and I attach landscaping fabric along the back, folding and stapling it so that the thick black material makes a pocket between each board.

It only takes about twenty minutes to make one. But by the time we've made six, we're all ready for a break. Jasper props each one up along Grampa's garage.

"Now how are we going to get them there?" I ask.

Mom smiles. "It's taken care of," she says as a bright yellow truck rumbles into Grampa's driveway.

"Archie!" I run over to give Archie a hug. "I didn't know you were coming."

"I wouldn't miss it." Archie's wearing a button-up and cardigan with dark dress shoes. He glances over at Mom and whispers, "Though I may be a bit overdressed."

I laugh as Mom and Jasper begin to load Archie's truck with all our pallets. After a quick stop by the garden supply store, we head over to Whispering Pines.

Jasper's mom and a few of the nurses come out and help us carry each pallet through the first floor and lean them up against the fence in the garden area. Then Mom, Jasper, and I get to work filling them with soil while Archie goes up to the second floor to distract Grampa and his new friends with leftover donuts.

Mom clenches her hands under her chin, takes in a huge breath, and looks at what we've made. "Well, I better go get him." She gives me a little nudge with her hip. "He's going to love it."

The French horn now holds a big mound of purple ornamental cabbage and sits nestled in a corner, and a few of the teapot planters are centerpieces on the tables. Jasper's mom worked everything out with the administrators of Whispering Pines; they even gave us some money for plants. We couldn't bring Grampa's whole yard, but what's important is it feels the same.

When the double doors open, it's not just Grampa. Mr. Curtis pushes Mrs. Wingfield, and Grampa and Toni walk in holding hands and make their way over to where Jasper and I stand. Then staff members and residents file out, and before long it seems like the whole second floor is there.

I point to the pallets. "It's called vertical gardening. There's no need for much digging or bending over really, so it's easier on the back and knees. We can add more pallets in the spring, but I checked at the garden store and there are a few things that will grow all through an Oklahoma winter." I motion to the plants. "Carrots, radishes, white potatoes, and onions."

I've never seen Grampa cry, but he wipes his cheek as he steps forward and wraps me in a hug. Grampa nods toward Mrs. Wingfield, who's wheeled over to a pallet with Mr. Curtis and already started working on a row of radishes. Grampa sniffles a little and says, "You know, this place, and my new friends, they can't replace your gramma. But it's been a long time since I've been this happy."

I swallow hard. "I don't think I was worried about Gramma being replaced. I know it's silly, but I thought without our treasure hunts, that maybe I was."

Grampa shakes his head. "Not possible. Nothing in this whole world could do that." He hugs me again before saying, "What you've done today is special. It lets us share something we love with everyone here." He looks over at Mom. "I think maybe we both kept too much to ourselves."

After a while, the staff brings out coffee and tea, and people settle at tables while some work on planting.

Toni sits next to Grampa, with Archie on his other side. Mom and Jasper sit next to me.

"You know what I was thinking?" Grampa says. "We maybe can't do the dumpster dives anymore, but what about garage sales? Now that I'm approved for day passes, I could help. Plus, the really good stuff goes fast. Sometimes, you have to get there before the sun is up. You know what that means?"

I smile and so does Grampa. "Headlamps!" we say at the same time, and everyone laughs.

Grampa points to each of us sitting around the table and then to himself. "With all of us searching, who knows what treasures await."

I look at our pallets, some already planted and peppered with green sprouts, and think about all of us sitting there together, all connected by this moment. I close my eyes and take a deep breath, and I don't have to open my heart to see if anything calls to it. For once, I feel like my heart has found everything it needs.

ACKNOWLEDGMENTS

If it hadn't been for some heart finds of my own, this book would still be an unfinished draft. In 2019, I was working on an unlikely friendship story between a grandparent and a girl who struggled to connect with her peers, but I couldn't quite get the story to work. Then I came across a video (posted by my wonderful editor) showing members of Abbington Senior Living performing a dance routine to Michael Jackson's "Thriller," and I knew what was missing—not just a single scene but a bigger sense of community and the idea of finding joy in unexpected places. So firstly, thank you to those seniors for bringing me joy that day and providing the thread that eventually helped me tie this story together. Traci Tullius and Katrina Muir, I'm convinced that stories of your grampa had nestled somewhere in my subconscious and slowly developed over the years into what was the original seed idea for this book. So, thank you, both—not so much for the idea, but for making me feel like a part of the Tullius family. Collomia Charles, Gigi Collins, Ellen Mulholland, and Siva Ramakrishnan, without the four of you this book would not be here; your early feedback gave this story and its author the boost they both needed. I'm forever indebted to my agent, Kaitlyn Johnson, who read an early draft in a single afternoon and convinced me it wasn't, as Mabel might say, a dud. I couldn't do it without you and your support! Samantha Gentry, editor extraordinaire, with each round of edits your input made this story so much better. To get to work with you on another book was a dream come true, and I hope there are many more to come! Thank you to cover designer Karina Granda and illustrator Oriol Vidal, who together created a cover that once again brought me to tears the first time I saw it and brought Mabel and Abner, Oklahoma, to life. I'm so grateful to the entire team at Little, Brown Books for Young Readers, with special thanks to Marisa Finkelstein, Jane Cavolina, Olivia Davis, Bill Grace, Mara Brashem,

Hannah Klein, and Christie Michel. Last but far from least, a huge thank-you to my family, who listened to me both complain and rejoice through each step of this whole process and did so with kindness, love, and patience. I love you, Chris, Owen, Sam, and Henry.

JAIME BERRY

is the author of *Hope Springs* and a native of rural Oklahoma. After years with two small boys in a too-small Brooklyn apartment, Jaime and her husband moved to the wilds of suburban New Jersey and added another boy and a dog to the mix. She invites you to visit her at jaimeberryauthor.com or follow her on Twitter @jaime_berry3.